Northern Ireland

Edited By Jenni Harrison

First published in Great Britain in 2019 by:

 Young**Writers**® — Est. 1991 —

Young Writers
Remus House
Coltsfoot Drive
Peterborough
PE2 9BF
Telephone: 01733 890066
Website: www.youngwriters.co.uk

★ Foreword

Dear Reader,

You will never guess what I did today! Shall I tell you? Some primary school pupils wrote some diary entries and I got to read them, and they were EXCELLENT!

They wrote them in school and sent them to us here at Young Writers. We'd given their teachers some bright and funky worksheets to fill in, and some fun and fabulous (and free) resources to help spark ideas and get inspiration flowing.

And it clearly worked because WOW!! I can't believe the adventures I've been reading about. Real people, make-believe people, dogs and unicorns, even objects like pencils all feature and these diaries all have one thing in common – they are JAM-PACKED with imagination!

We live and breathe creativity here at Young Writers – it gives us life! We want to pass our love of the written word onto the next generation and what better way to do that than to celebrate their writing by publishing it in a book!

It sets their work free from homework books and notepads and puts it where it deserves to be – OUT IN THE WORLD! Each awesome author in this book should be **super proud** of themselves, and now they've got proof of their imagination, their ideas and their creativity in black and white, to look back on in years to come!

Now that I've read all these diaries, I've somehow got to pick some winners! Oh my gosh it's going to be difficult to choose, but I'm going to have SO MUCH FUN doing it!

Bye!

Jenni

Contents

Livia Alice Whelan (10)	92
Beth Devaney (10)	94
Emily Fulton (10)	96
Emelia McGeown (10)	97
Tyler Campbell (11)	98
Ava-Grace Shaw (11)	99
Katie Kirkpatrick (10)	100

Creavery Primary School, Antrim

Lewis Millar Nimick (10)	101
Daisy Thompson (10)	102
Lea Williamson (11)	104
Hannah Quinn (11)	106
Emily Adair (11)	107
Phoebe Grace Caldwell (10)	108
Louise Hill (10)	109
Megan Bremner (10)	110
Ben Alexander McCosh (11)	111
Maggie Jayne Ellis (10)	112
Willow Dawson (11)	113
Samuel Craig (11)	114
Lucas Millar (11)	115
Gracie Alexa Rose Doran (11)	116

Ebrington Primary School, Londonderry

Claire McClements (10)	117
James Smallwoods (10)	118
Hollie Thomas (11)	121
Rihanna Borland (11)	122
Catherine Campbell (10)	124
Bonnie McQue (11)	126
Brooke Margaret Bridget Kerr (10)	128
Tristyn Nathan Taggart (9)	130
Riley Kennedy (10)	132
Holly Nicole Clifford (11)	134
Sienna Faye Campbell (11)	136
Dylan McPoyle (11)	138
Christian Patterson (11)	140
Ben Campbell Haslett (11)	142
Anna Curtis (11)	144

Armani Mitchell (9)	146
Eloise Catherine White (9)	148
Ben McKnight (10)	150
Jason Patterson (11)	152
Amelia Doherty (10)	154
Brandon Gleed (11)	156
Hannah Brown (11)	157
Jessica Hockley-Crockett (10)	158
Hazel Stephanie Louise Hamilton (10)	159
Kizzy Harvey (10)	160
Cameron McArthur (10)	162

Gaelscoil Na Móna, Belfast

Tierna Cora Power (10)	163
Angela-Louise Conlon (11)	165
David McDermott (11)	167
Cassierose McCoubrey (10)	169
Chloe Martin (10)	171
Kyla McVeigh (11)	173

Rathcoole Primary School, Newtownabbey

Ellen Archer (10)	175
Ella Conroy (11)	176
Erin Lee McKibbin (9)	177
Brandon Rice (10)	178

St Macartan's Primary School, Clogher

Niall McKenna (10)	179
Mairéad McConnell (11)	180
Crystal Condy (11)	182
Tiarnán Meehan (10)	183

St Patrick's Primary School, Maghera

Emma Rose Convery (9)	184
Jim Holloway (9)	186
Fionn Wallace (8)	188
Daniel O'Kane (9)	189

Méabh Donoghue (8)	190
Cara Holloway (9)	191
Annie McKenna (9)	192
CiCi Murray (8)	193
Jason Bradley (9)	194
Patrick Bradley (9)	195
Owen Glass (8)	196
Meghan O'Kane (8)	197

St Tierney's Primary School, Roslea

Grace Connolly (9)	198
Anna Rooney (9)	200
Aodhan O'Donnell (8)	202

Thornfield House School, Newtownabbey

Brooklyn Fisher (10)	203
Abbie Savage (10)	204
Zak Patterson (9)	206
Maksims Andrejevs (10)	207
Jake Whitehouse (9)	208
Ethan Mulholland (10)	209
Mason Bowers (9)	210
Marley Sebastian Ludew (10)	211

The Diaries

Ocean Adventures

Dear Diary,

What's the point in living beside a beach if your mum won't let you swim? She says it's because Dad drowned... Uhh! I don't care anymore, I am going in the water.

I ran towards the water but then stopped. It was freezing. My legs felt like jelly. I fell over. I tried to stand up but looked back at my legs and there was a tail.

"Argh!" I started screaming like mad. I tried to get out of the water. I felt like I was getting pulled in. I tried to get up for air but realised I could breathe. I was swimming and it was my first time in the water. I swam around. I saw coral and fish. I saw caves and rocks. It was awesome. Then I swam further. The most surprising thing I saw was... a merman! He turned around to look at me. My jaw dropped. It was my Dad who had drowned two years ago. I started crying as he swam towards me and hugged me. After that we swam back to the beach. My mum was looking for me. When me and Dad got out of the water, he explained everything. Also, I was only a mermaid in the water. So my life is normal except when I am in the water.

Beth Cartin (11)
Balloughry Primary School, Balloughry

The Secret Treasure Chest

Dear Diary,

Today I invited my friends over to my house and they're called Siobhan, Holly, Caoimhe, Chanice and Beth. We all went to my attic to play. Me and Beth were messing around and accidentally knocked a picture off the wall so we went to see what it was. Holly picked it up and said, "It's a map!"

Siobhan said, "It is really?"

"Yes it is!"

I said, "Well we know what to do then. Let's go!"

"Yippee!" said Caoimhe.

"Are you out of your mind?" said Holly.

"I'm going," I said.

Siobhan, Beth and Caoimhe all agreed to go. We followed the map and we walked for hours. Eventually, we reached a cave. We heard shouting coming from it.

"W-w-what's that?" said Beth.

"Boo!" We all screamed. It was Holly.

"Where did you come from?"

"I followed you but Chanice had to go."

"Well shall we go in?" I said. We all went in.
Then Holly said, "What's that shining inside?" it
was a chest and it was treasure, gold and silver
coins. We grabbed as much as we could and ran
home.

Ebony Griffin (11)

Ballougry Primary School, Ballougry

The Life Of A Sword

Dear Diary,
We have started our journey to Niflheim, it is going to take us a long time to get there...

Dear Diary,
It has been a week since we left. I would have written here the day after we left but I was in pendant form.

Dear Diary,
It's been two weeks. We lost three men fighting spies, but we still have seventeen men left. We met up with another group of Einherjar/Einherji. We were about 100 miles away from the battle and we found a raided giant camp. We found another group of Einherjar/Einherji.

Dear Diary,
It has been two months since we left and there are about fifty miles to go. About twenty-five miles away from the main battle we also found the Olympians, so I might have a date with Riptide soon.

Dear Diary,
Five miles away from the battle so I might be gone for quite a while. Sorry, I have to go now.

Dear Diary,
We have been fighting for a month now, but we made them retreat after Riptide and I defeated Surt.

Dear Diary,
So it has been a year since we won, Riptide and I have had plenty of dates.

Cormac Clarke (10)
Ballougry Primary School, Ballougry

Onyx Black Bomb Queen

Dear Diary,

It's only seven days, 3.25 hours and 122 seconds until... the bomb goes off over NYC! The boss says, if it works, I'll be promoted. Imagine, youngest ever Super Spy for IHORB! Michelle called, or, sorry, Miss Windsor called. #meanboss. She was never eager to promote me but Alexis Milan (president of IHORB) thinks I have potential! Gotta go! Bomb in two days and one hour! Can hardly sleep! It goes off in six hours. I am leaving to go to IHORB main agency for the first time ever!

Dear Diary,

I can hardly write, it all went so wrong! I arrived at IHORB, walked into reception, made myself a coffee to realise I was late! I ran from the building to the beach. Guess who was there? Michelle! She didn't want me to get promoted because she didn't want me to be hooked on the bad spy thing like she was. You see, she's Alexis' sister! I've decided now, after getting shot at and after all the blood, sweat and tears, I don't want to be a spy anymore. But it will take a bit of letting go!

Holly Hutcheon (11)

Ballougry Primary School, Ballougry

The Mission To Find A Friend

7th March, 2019

Dear Diary,

My name is Bob the alien I have no friends, but today I went to Earth to make some friends. I was very nervous. What if they didn't like me? Well, I got on my spaceship and made my way to Earth. I was less than a metre away from Earth, but everyone was screaming. They were probably just excited to see me. But when I landed, there were these people that had lasers and they were wearing blue. I went up to them and said the least scary thing I could think of, which was, "I come in peace!"

Then they started to shoot me with their lasers. I ran to my spaceship, but I still needed a friend. I saw this person laughing, so I grabbed him and took him with me. When I got in my UFO I saw a lady crying. She must want a friend too. I knew how she felt so I took the little person out of my UFO and gave him to the lady. Then the lady said, "Thank you."

I said, "Will you be my friend?"

The lady said, "Yes, will you live with me?"

Chlöe Carrie Alison Duncan-Stevenson (10)

Ballougry Primary School, Ballougry

The Incredible Diary Of... The Unicorn

7th March, 2019

Dear Diary,

One morning I got up and went outside to the beach. I dipped my feet in the water and it was freezing! I heard a sound and I turned around. There was a... unicorn!

I was so surprised. I couldn't believe my eyes! I went over to it so it looked at me and then started licking me! It was white and its hair was pink, purple and blue. I said hello. It said, "Hi, what is your name?"

I said, "My name is Ava. What is yours?"

She said she didn't have a name so I told her I would name her. She said she had a hut on the beach so we went there. I called her Lola. A few weeks later, we were best friends!

One day we were having a water fight but Lola didn't like it. When I threw some water at her, she screamed, "Stop!"

I got a fright and ran away. I went back home, ran up to my room and watched a movie.

I went back to the beach and she was there. We said sorry to each other and became friends again.

Ava Loughran (9)

Ballougry Primary School, Ballougry

The Incredible Diary Of... Spider-Man

Dear Diary,

I can't even believe today. I was bitten by a spider! Not just a spider, a radioactive spider, which changed my DNA. Well, here's what happened.

Our school went to Oscorp and we had a guide. The guide showed us the spiders.

He said, "These are radioactive spiders and there are 100 spiders."

One of the girls from my class said, "There's only 99 spiders."

The guide replied, "Oh no!"

Then I felt something tickling my hand. Then something bit me. I looked and it was the missing spider. After the lab, we had to go back and do a science quiz about what we had learned. I didn't know anything! But Flash (the school bully) went to throw a ball at me and my head was tingling, so I ducked. Flash's ball hit the teacher on the head.

I thought, *my DNA is better like this.*

So I made a costume and mask. I am not just Peter Parker, I'm Spider-Man and I fight crime and bad guys. So watch out!

Ronan Rutherford (11)

Ballougry Primary School, Ballougry

The Incredible Diary Of... The Hamster Gizmo

8th March, 2019

Dear Diary,

One morning, I woke up so happy because I was getting a hamster that day. So, first we went to the pet store and bought a two-storey cage. Then I bought a hamster and he was so cute. Then we got a hamster ball so it could run around. Then we went to my house and I fed him. Then we went to bed.

The next morning, I put him in the ball and he went crazy. That morning, when he was in his ball, he peed in it and it went all over the ground. I took so long to clean it up. He was a Russian hamster. He said, "I want to go outside my ball."

I said no, we would go out tomorrow because it said on the weather forecast that it was going to be sunny tomorrow. The next morning it was snowing! The forecast was wrong! I said, "Sorry Gizmo, we can't go out."

He said, "Well, can we play in the snow?"

I said okay. So I put him in his ball and we went out to play. Gizmo said it was really good fun.

Lucas Vafias (10)

Ballougry Primary School, Ballougry

10

The Silly Wish

Dear Diary,

I am so bored today. Mum told me to tidy my room but I can't be bothered. I think I will go for a walk with my dog Felix seeing as it's sunny outside.

Okay, we've been walking for a while, so I decide to rest by a rock. I notice Felix is sniffing something near a bush. I don't think much of it at first because all dogs do that. But now, he isn't even responding to me when I call him. I go to have a look at what he is sniffing. It's a necklace. It is really pretty so I decide to keep it.

We've walked back home now and I'm really bored again. I'm just moping around looking for something fun to do. I wish I could be somewhere else, like go to a different world.

Now I am freaking out! As I was writing the last sentence, the necklace started glowing and, now I'm in a weird place! I don't know what to do!

Dear Diary,

I've managed to escape. I'm so happy!

Leona Cole (11)

Ballougry Primary School, Ballougry

The Incredible Diary Of...

Dear Diary,

My name is Default Dan. I live in Pleasant Park. One of my hobbies is hiding in a bush. Anyway, my mystery began when I was out of food and needed to go down to Retail Row. On my way to Retail Row, I stopped to buy a burger in Tilted Towers. All of a sudden, I saw some TTV tryhards. One of them had a metal baseball bat.

The biggest one said, "Give me all your money and nobody gets hurt."

I was really scared so I stuttered, "O-okay."

They took all my money but I suddenly realised I still had my burger. Yay!

I then became best friends with my burger. We walked around Tilted Towers for a while, hiding in bushes along the way. That was fun.

On the way home, I found an epic John Wick guy beating up the TTV tryhards. He turned around and saw me and said, "Here's your money," and gave it to me.

I walked home and eventually ate my burger.

Aidan McBride (11)

Ballougry Primary School, Ballougry

12

Me In A Dog's Life

7th March 2019

Dear Diary,

Today has been the best day of my life. OMG! I just turned into a dog! Why? I don't know! I think because... My dog licked me? And now I don't have to go to school! Yay!

So, now I can talk to my dog. Weird I know. But still cool! But my mum gave me ice cream and I don't know if I should eat it? And then I found some chocolate, but I forgot, I'm a dog. So I had to go to the vet! Dun, dun, dun!

But thank goodness, I'm fine! Then we were going to the park. Yay!

But it was a dog park though. Alfie was barking a lot! He barks at everything he sees! Why? So we just went home because he was barking so much. When we got home, mum put me and Alfie in dog sweaters! Noooo! I hate this! But we did have a photoshoot, so I'm kind of happy, I guess. Bark! Bark!

I really hoped you liked my diary. Woof!

Molly Stevenson (10)

Ballougry Primary School, Ballougry

The Incredible Diary Of... A Banana

Dear Diary,

I am a banana. I have no idea how I found pen and paper small enough for me to write this. Anyway, today I escaped humans. Let me tell you how.

So, I was chilling with Apple in the fruit bowl and Apple was like, "I don't wanna be eaten so do you wanna escape?"

I said, "Yeah sure, let's do it." So we made an agreement that the best way out was the window. When the human left, I jumped out of the window first, ready to catch Apple. I saw the human behind Apple, just as he was ready to jump! The giant human had grabbed for Apple and took a huge bite out of him. Then, when the human wasn't looking (because it was getting a drink) Apple jumped out of the window after me.

After that we ran and ran and ran, until we found an abandoned farm with lots of other runaway fruit. We lived there for the rest of our lives.

Emily Wallace (10)

Ballougry Primary School, Ballougry

Moving On

Dear Diary,
I love my granny. She is the best. She helped me with my birthday party. Today was great. Everyone in school wished me a happy birthday and my birthday party was even better. Everyone came from school and they were saying that it was the best party ever!

Dear Diary,
Yesterday Mummy said that my granny had died. It has been a hard week. Today I walked up to my granny's house after swimming because I forgot.

Dear Diary,
My granny left me a message. It said that when she was a young girl, her granny told her that before she died she would get the meaning of life. She also left me a necklace.

Dear Diary,
I put on the necklace that my granny left me and it is really, really lucky. I am Miss Popular and, even better, there is a piece of my granny with me every day.

Caoimhe McGinley (11)
Ballougry Primary School, Ballougry

Alexa's Diary (The Cat)

Dear Diary,

I went to the park and saw a puppy. He said, "Why, hello there!"

"Hello," I said.

"Wanna be BFFs forever?" he said.

"Sure!" I said.

Two weeks later, I went back to the park. I realised he wasn't there. First, I thought he was just sick of all the bugs going round and round but then he didn't show up for a week.

Then I saw him. We ran to each other and he kissed me. Then we started dating and he proposed. After that we had kids. I told the kids how we met and they said they wanted to do the same. OMG! They're only five!

Annalise Hurl Platt (9)

Ballougry Primary School, Ballougry

Diary Of A Farm Vet

Dear Diary,

I was up at 4am today. I was lambing a ewe. She had triplets, but one died. That's life. I went back and had breakfast.

Two minutes later, I was sliding my hand in a cow's insides pulling out what was in there. It was a bull calf. I was lambing again two hours later for my dad. Then I went home and fed some cows. I looked in the sheep shed and a sheep was bleating. I got a glove and I felt triplets again. I got one out, then did it again. The other two were free. All three survived.

James Mackey (9)

Ballougry Primary School, Ballougry

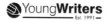

A Super Player

Dear Diary,

My name is Fintan Loughran and today my football team were in the final! Once the match began, we were on a roll! We scored the first goal! I scored the first goal and at half-time we were really happy. When it was the second half, no team scored so that meant we won! I got to lift the cup. When I did we all said, "Yes!" and we went running round the pitch shouting, "Winner!"

I could not believe that we'd won. You never know what you can win sometimes!

Fintan Loughran (10)

Ballougry Primary School, Ballougry

A Diary Entry By Angus

(Inspired by 'The Water Horse' by Dick King-Smith)

Dear Diary,

It has been one of those days! I thought it was going to be a normal day, but then something very, very unexpected happened. I was on the beach, climbing over the rocks, when I found a huge egg thing. I didn't know what you would call it. I left it for a while, just sitting about. And something mega happened! The egg cracked open and a creature popped out!

I went to find Kirstie to tell her about it. I spoke to Kirstie and we decided to put it in the bath full of blue, clear water. But then I had a super idea to put salt in the water to make it feel at home. But I guess the creature would need some food, so me and Kirstie tiptoed downstairs to get some food for the creature. We decided to feed it sardines. It gobbled them up as quick as a flash and settled down a little bit. We soon found out that it was called a kelpie! That is quite a weird name so we called it Crusoe. Crusoe started to get very jumpy but he soon settled down. I feel really tired, so I am

ending it here. This is a lot to take in but there will be more tomorrow.
See you later.
Angus

Evie Hughes (9)
Bocombra Primary School, Portadown

The Incredible Diary Of... The BFG

(Inspired by 'The BFG' by Roald Dahl)

Dear Diary,

Last night I is walking secretly around Englund blowing dreams into bedrooms when I is hearing the clumpety-clumpety-clump of a little chiddler's heartbeat across the road. Then I grabbed the chiddler out of its bed in the norphanage and grabbed my bag and ran down the road. I flew across the world to Giant Country and landed on the dry ground. Then I sprinted to my cave and rolled the stone back and walked inside.

I set the chiddler on my desk and asked it its name. She is called Sophie and is a norphan. She is telling me that she will have to go back but she can't or else she'll go telling everyone about giants, though I told her woppsy-big-secrets about the dream-catching. She said she is not telling a soul. So I gave her a snozzcumber but she hated it and spat it all over the table.

We talked about dreams some more and then I showed her the other giants. They is all lying on the ground snoring. Sophie said they looked utterly disgusting, so we went back inside.

Sophie asked about where dreams come from but I said it was time for bed. So she slept in a matchbox.
From BFG

Jack Cousins (10)
Bocombra Primary School, Portadown

The BFG's Human Friend
(Inspired by 'The BFG' by Roald Dahl)

Dear Diary,

Yesterday, I was walking down the streets when I see a little chidler taking a peeksy at me while I is blowing dreams! The human bean did try to hide from me but I is not missing nothing! I do take her to Giant Country. When me and her get to me hometown, she does question me speaking! I is very offended. She did give me pains in me tummywinkle. Ow!

I do tell her that I is having to do me job but she is such a noseybonkle that I is not allowed to go any place without her! It doesn't know what's out there! We do get outside and she did see me worst friends! Bloodbottler, Frogglehumper and, of course, Fleshlumpeater. We do sneak past them and get to me job which is... dream-catching! Actually, I do think it is the only job you can get in Giant Country but don't mind that.

Why hello there Diary, I is now reading the chidler a story when she says that she doesn't dream. Nonsense! Everyone dreams! At least I think so. Since I is the smartest giant you will meet, I does decide to give her a bad dream with me trumpet. It

is about me doing a whizzpopper in her face. That should teach her.
Bye.
The BFG

Annie Hamilton (10)

Bocombra Primary School, Portadown

My Amazing Diary Entry
(Inspired by 'The Water Horse' by Dick King-Smith)

Dear Diary,

I can't wait to tell you all about what happened today! This morning, when I woke up, me and Kirstie went to the bathroom. I thought we were getting breakfast! I was disappointed honestly, but then I saw a monster in the bathtub. We gave it sardines, he seemed to like them! I wanted to share the sardines, but Kirstie is bossy! "Don't do this, don't do that!" Shiver me timbers! I wish she would stop talking! I was thinking of tough monster names, but we decided on Crusoe, like Robinson Crusoe for the monster. All monsters need names. I'm currently brushing my teeth, beside Crusoe. Well... I'm not, I'll stop writing to do so.

I'm back. Crusoe tried to eat my toothpaste so I had to rush to my bed. Now Grumble is happy that all of this happened. It's odd, I've never seen him like this before. Anyway! I hope that Crusoe grows into a huge, *huge* monster! So he can touch the clouds and I can ride him. It would be so cool! I can imagine it in the newspapers! 'Boy touches clouds with his own barc hands!'

Today was a very strange day. I wonder what tomorrow will bring?
Angus

Cora Frazer (8)
Bocombra Primary School, Portadown

The Story Of Urrtork The Viking

19th March, 866

Dear Diary,

I have an urge to go out raiding, but as soon as I mention it to my wife, Mary, I always hear the same reply, "No Urrtork, I am going to have a child and I will need you." As you see, I will be cooped up in here until Mary has the baby.

22nd March, 866

Dear Diary,

Guess what just happened, it is marvellous! Mary had her baby! It is a girl, so she won't go on a raid quite so soon. We called her Nora.

19th March, 869

Dear Diary,

A lot has happened and sadly, not the best for me. Here it is. I went with the other Vikings on the raid. They were all happy and jolly and, well I suppose, I was too, for a time. I felt the usual pride and honour of being a returning raider and this was time number four.

The monastery came into view. Then we ran through the seas and onto the beach. In the battle, I lost one of my arms. It was horrible but at least it wasn't my head!

19th March, 870
Dear Diary,
This is the last entry you will receive as I am nearly
out of carving pages. I have had a hard time but
you have always been here for me. Nora is now
four and is a great help to Mary. I now must say,
goodbye.

Kathryn Gault (9)
Bocombra Primary School, Portadown

The Tale Of Asgard The Bold

An extract

Dear Diary,

Although I haven't written to you for a while, there have been some entertaining events that I need to remember. So, there I was, enjoying the salty sea air on my face, feeling free. Of course, I was doing my job on the lookout. We all had our armour and shields with us, just in case there was a surprise attack. I was beginning to give up hope about ever finding a 'better land' until, "Land ahoy!" I shouted with all my might.

We all cheered. I felt like the champion I once was, even with a small victory. After quite a while of smooth sailing, we hit a rock and we knew we'd hit land. We were going for a sneak attack. So when we saw a group of monks we all wanted to cheer but, as I said, we were going for a sneak attack. So we grabbed each monk one by one and forced them to tell us where we were and where their goods were. They told us we were in Jorvik in England. We managed to steal all the monks' gold. Soon after, I decided monks weren't enough. I wanted something their country really loved. After thinking for a while, I got it... their king!

When I got to the grand palace, there were guards. I mean, who'd have thought? So not really Viking style getting thrown in jail by guards and being told that you're going to be beheaded the next day...

Daisy Guy (9)
Bocombra Primary School, Portadown

Some Days In The Diary Of Kiki Peltzer

Dear Diary,

Kiki Peltzer here! On 7th November, it was my seventh birthday and my father finally let me practise sword fighting! My new sword has Thor's hammer on it because my father thought Thor was my favourite god - but he isn't. Loki is my favourite, but I didn't tell my father that because everyone in the village's favourite god is supposed to be Thor because of tradition or something. Anyway, after about five minutes of practising, my father (the chief) said I was the best swordfighter in Norway!

A few hours later, my dog, Dublin died. I was very, very sad, but he had been my mum's dog for seven years before mine so he was fourteen. I think that means he was eighty-four in dog years, but anyway I was really sad.

On 8th November, my father went out to war but little did he know I was going with him. I had to sneak into a spare chest and someone put me on the ship. Thank Odin for that! My legs were starting to get sore, and the chest kept moving because the waves got really high! Anyway, Valkar took me to my father where he shouted at me for ages!

After my father's tantrum, he said he was kind of proud of me because I had been able to sneak on the boat without anyone noticing me!
Anyway, we arrived in a place called Ireland. The battle went on for hours when we finally... won!

Emily Matchett (10)

Bocombra Primary School, Portadown

A Diary Entry By Grumble

(Inspired by 'The Water Horse' by Dick King-Smith)

Thursday, 14th March

Dear Diary,

Today started off just as an ordinary day but then I got quite a shock and surprise. When I woke up I walked into the bathroom to go to the loo and, to my surprise, I found Kirstie and Angus feeding a strange creature my expensive sardines in the bath. I was about to scream and screech but then they started to explain the whole story. When they finished telling me the story, I was okay with this whole scandal and told them it was maybe a sea monster! Angus and Kirstie did not agree, they thought it was just a kelpie.

After that, we just chatted for a while and I spoke to them about keeping this secret from Mum. She'd just flip if she found out! But, of course, she just walked into the bathroom and said, "I'm not surprised!"

The room was silent for a moment until Angus shouted, "It's a kelpie!"

"Yes, I know that Angus," said Mum. For a while, we talked about the name and we decided Crusoe. Crusoe is a lovely name, everyone thought.

Me and Mum decided, since Crusoe was growing lots, we are going to let him live in the goldfish pond. It was a brilliant idea. Kirstie and Angus thought so too. It was a brilliant idea, so much excitement and joy but it's getting late now and I must go to bed. I'll write again soon.
Grumble

Zoe Clarke (9)
Bocombra Primary School, Portadown

Sophie's Diary

(Inspired by 'The BFG' by Roald Dahl)

Dear Diary,

I was lying in bed and I couldn't sleep. I got out of bed. I suddenly remembered that was the hour that was called the witching hour. I was trying very hard to get to sleep, but I couldn't! There was a giant moonbeam shining on my pillow.

All the other children in the room were fast asleep. I put my glasses on because I can hardly see without them. I looked behind the curtain. Suddenly, I saw this big giant black thing coming up the road. It was very tall. It was very thin. I knew it couldn't be a human, it was far too big for that.

After a while, I realised what it was doing. It stopped in each window in nearly every house. It bent down to look in.

Things happened very quickly after that. It came closer and closer to my window and suddenly, a giant hand reached in! I was terrified. It grabbed me, blanket and everything. It started running very fast. I figured out that it must be a giant! It ran so fast, I could feel it lifting off the ground.

We arrived at this land that I had never heard of before. I couldn't see much because I was too scared to look. When the giant finally stopped, I peeked out. We were in something like a house. A very big one. I was terrified of being eaten alive, but when I said so, he laughed hysterically. "Me eating human beans? Never!" he laughed.

Niomi Richardson (9)
Bocombra Primary School, Portadown

The Diary Of Odean

Dear Diary,

I was stupid. I don't know why I was looking forward to my first raid. I have been seasick overboard nine times and once on Davide's hair. I have not seen any other ships yet and the sun has been resting behind the wispy clouds. We have not seen it for five days and the navigator has been finding it hard to find our way through the dense fog. On the positive side though, we have breezed through the waters with ease as there have been no storms since the first night aboard.

Now we are nearing land. The chief has been bellowing orders to us a lot recently so that we don't get blown off course by the choppy seas. We cruised through the seas and landed on the island. A towering monastery stood in front of us. We had some monks to kill!

We have enslaved some monks and killed the rest and we are homeward bound on our longship. We have piles of riches and 'godly' ornaments. Lots of Thor-like symbols that, for some reason, the 'holy people' turn around so they are facing upwards, are overflowing in everyone's chests.

But we have seen something incredibly dangerous. Progressing towards us is an odd-looking ship. It is pretty unique compared to ours. It has artistic decorations carved professionally into the wood like ours does and is taller. Now they are on our vessel. Argh! I'm petrified!

Kaeden Curran (10)

Bocombra Primary School, Portadown

Matilda's Best Day!
(Inspired by 'Matilda' by Roald Dahl)

Dear Diary,

Hello, I am Matilda. I have a terrible mother, father and even a terrible brother! They treat me like I am not their daughter! I usually read books in my room and ignore my parents. I have always wanted to go to school and my wish came true! My dad, called Mr Wormwood, went into my pink room, full of books and said that he was fed up with me! I was so excited! I got up from my pink bed and got changed. I did my hair and put on a pretty red ribbon.

After I got ready, I got my black bag and got in the car. When my dad pushed me out of the car, harshly, I ran as fast as a hare to the school. We were waiting patiently and eventually we went inside. I was walking around the huge school and saw a lonely girl. I was really eager to ask if she was alright. She was alright so I asked her if she wanted to be my friend. She said yes. I asked her what her name was. She said it was Lavender. I told her my name is Matilda.

At school, we all saw the horrible Miss Trunchbull. We walked as quietly as a mouse.

At class, we all saw Miss Honey. I felt safe with her. Miss Trunchbull made me feel scared. Miss Honey was a kind and pretty lady. We did our quiz and I got full marks! At break and lunch, I usually play with Lavender. At class, Miss Trunchbull randomly came inside and put me in the chokey. Eventually, after three hours I got out.

Maria Jessica Almendral (9)

Bocombra Primary School, Portadown

Matilda's Normal School Day

(Inspired by 'Matilda' by Roald Dahl)

Dear Diary,

Today has been the most horrible day of my life because when I woke up, my parents were shouting at me like mad. They were tired from last night. They didn't let me have my favourite breakfast, instead they made me eat beans on toast, which I hate so much.

When I got to school, I saw Miss Trunchbull and I got extremely nervous that she would shout at me. She didn't. I was really happy that she didn't. When we all got to class, I saw Miss Honey and she looked gorgeous in her new purple dress. We all had to go to assembly and I saw someone a lot older than me doodling Miss Trunchbull. She saw it and the person who did it got put in the chokey - that was very scary.

When it was lunchtime, we got to go first and get our lunch and it was absolutely disgusting. It was all lumpy and sloppy. After that, I felt like I was going to be sick. After lunch we had to go back to class and Miss Trunchbull came to inspect us because she thought we were up to something extremely strange that we should not be doing.

After school, when I got home, I had to do my homework. After that, I really wanted to go outside but my parents wouldn't let me. I kept saying I really wanted to go outside and finally, they let me. At dinner they made me eat microwave food in front of the TV which I hate.

Finally, after a long day I went to bed. I wonder what my adventure is going to be tomorrow?

Riley Marney (10)
Bocombra Primary School, Portadown

The Incredible Diary Of...

Dear Diary,

This has been a regretful, remarkable, horrid and hungry day! You see, yesterday, when I was helping Mother do the housework, a sudden idea struck me as I looked out of the window and watched the men, including my father, bring all of their possessions onto the newly-built longboat. Tomorrow (now today) they were going to set sail on a voyage which would probably last for months on end. They were going trading, exploring and, maybe, raiding. Those three things they were going to do I would have loved to be a part of. Well, maybe not the raiding. So a plan began to form in my mind and, at moonlight, I went quietly onto the longboat and hid in one of the sacks of food. Along with me I brought my diary, some food and my favourite amber necklace Mother had given me. Now the men have come on the longboat and set sail and, believe me, it is so uncomfortable sitting in this sack. I hope they don't discover me!

This has been a horrific day. The men suddenly decided to go trading in Sweden but then secretly they are going to get revenge on the Swedish for capturing my sister, Friggel. They never told anyone in Ireland they were going to Sweden!

43

As soon as they left, some Swedish men came on the boat, thought the sack I was in was a goods one and opened it up and discovered me! Now I'm locked in a secret cupboard in one of their houses. I am going to stop writing now because I can hear them coming. Please! Someone help me!

Evie Thompson (10)
Bocombra Primary School, Portadown

The Best Day Of My Life
(Inspired by 'Matilda' by Roald Dahl)

Dear Diary,

Today I had a terrific first day of school. When I began school, it was horrible. First of all, I wanted to go to school but Mr and Mrs Wormwood would not let me - they are my parents. My grumpy parents didn't pay any attention to me and I didn't shout, I just stayed quiet. I turned the old television off and they got extremely cross.

Eventually, they brought me as quick as a flash to a wonderful school called Carriblack Primary School. I met a lovely teacher called Miss Honey. I also met Lavender and Nigel, they are my best friends.

Later on, I met a horrendous woman called Miss Trunchbull. She came in to our classroom and threw a friendly boy out of the upstairs window and he flew with an uncomfortable landing. Miss Trunchbull turned around and said to all of us not to mess with her. Miss Trunchbull stomped out of our wonderful classroom and slammed the door closed so hard.

I stood up on top of my desk and told everyone that I would not accept this behaviour and that I want to become the beautiful queen of the school. I magically threw Miss Trunchbull out of a window

and that is payback for what she did to that boy. I finally got control of the school forever. Every happy child cheered delightedly and Miss Trunchbull was never to be seen again. That evening as I was standing outside my terrible house, my brother Michael became my superhero sidekick and now my parents obey me because Miss Honey made them obey me. I hope that every day will be like this one.

Joel Eakins (9)
Bocombra Primary School, Portadown

A Diary Entry By Angus
(Inspired by 'The Water Horse' by Dick King-Smith)

Thursday, 14th March

Dear Diary,

You won't believe what happened to me today! It turned out to be such a super day! I found a very weird creature. I wasn't scared at all! When I found it, I tiptoed as quiet as a mouse, to the bathroom. No one saw me so then I had a very good look at it, it was very strange. So then I ran to the bath so I could put it in some water. The creature looked very hungry and I was hungry too. But I didn't know what the creature should eat so I went to get my big sister, Kirstie. When Kirstie saw the creature she was so shocked about what I had brought home. Then I said to her not to tell anyone. She said okay. She said we should feed it sardines. So I went quickly to the fridge to fetch them. Then I ran as quick as lightning up the creaky stairs and went to the bathroom again. So me and Kirstie fed it to him and I ate some too! Then I heard Mum say, "Where are the sardines?"

I told her I ate some and had to bring the rest back to the fridge. I thought for a few seconds and decided we needed some help. I told Kirstie that I thought we needed help. She agreed. So I thought we should get Grumble, our grandad. So I said that

47

to Kirstie but she thought it was a bad idea because Grumble might tell Mum. So we had to look after the creature ourselves. I said to Kirstie, "What if Mum and Dad find out?"
Kirstie said, "Why do you think that?"
I said, "Because Mum takes a bath every Friday night!"
Now I have to go to bed. I will write to you soon.
Angus

Heidi Alderdice (9)
Bocombra Primary School, Portadown

A Diary Entry By Kirstie!
(Inspired by 'The Water Horse' by Dick King-Smith)

Thursday, 14th March

Dear Diary,

You won't believe what happened to me! It was such an amazing day! It was a stormy night so I could *not* sleep! I could hear the wind outside and it was super, mega loud. I tried to look on the bright side and thought maybe we could go beachcombing. I finally got to sleep.

When we went beachcombing the next day, I found something that looked like a mermaid's purse! My grumpy old granda Grumble said it was a big old piece of seaweed. I brought it home anyway and only told my little brother Angus about it. Angus said to put it in a bucket of water. So we did. And then Angus said to put salt in the bucket and I thought that was an incredible idea! We went to sleep quite early because we thought if we slept, it might hatch! I woke up at midnight and peeped through the door where the bucket was and it was just floating there. I whispered to myself, "You're stupid!" and went back to bed. When I woke up it had hatched! I thought it was a monster! I told Angus and he ran as fast as those little legs of his could go. We decided to put it in the bath now that it was bigger.

"It looks hungry," I said to Angus, so we tried to feed it lots of different things but it wouldn't eat them.

Angus said, "What about sardines?" So we tried sardines and it ate them. Suddenly, Grumble came in! We tried to hide the bath but he still saw.

"Is this what I think it is?" said Grumble. "A kelpie!" Anyway, talk to you soon. I have to go to bed now. Bye.

Kirstie

Isabella Best (9)

Bocombra Primary School, Portadown

The Worst Day Ever
(Inspired by 'Matilda' by Roald Dahl)

Wednesday, 27th March 1978

Dear Diary,

When I woke up, my horrendous family were all glued to the TV eating their unhealthy breakfast. My awful mummy decided to give me nothing! I was as mad as a crazy bull.

After that, I got changed into beautiful clothes. I thought I was so pretty when I looked in the enormous mirror in my tiny little room. Now I was ready to leave my lazy family to go to my new school, Crunchem Hall, which is humungous.

When I finally arrived at my new school, I was terribly nervous. I had never been in a building as big as it before. A kind and young teacher, called Miss Honey, came quickly towards me. She was hopping like a bunny rabbit and this had me a little terrified. She then brought me to a lovely classroom with lots of friendly kids sitting quietly. After a while, I got introduced to the whole class. I sat beside a beautiful girl called Lavender. Lavender and I became besties. To me, the work we did wasn't even a little bit hard.

When it was nearly time to go home, I left and before I could go much further, Miss Trunchbull charged towards me and picked me up like I was a bag or something. After that she just threw me over an enormous, creepy fence. It took me ages to get back out, but I eventually did.

When I arrived back to my disgusting house, my brother Michael was the only annoying person there. Thoughtfullym I decided to leave. So I set off to a quiet place called a library. I absolutely love to read so that place was heavenly to me. An old lady, Mrs Phelps, helped me pick a book that she knew I would love. She is like a best friend to me. Matilda

Gracie McNeill (9)
Bocombra Primary School, Portadown

The BFG's Terrific Plan

(Inspired by 'The BFG' by Roald Dahl)

Dear Diary,

I'm sorry I haven't written more over this stretch of time. It was because something really weird happened two nights ago.

I was doing what I do every night, blowing dreams, good or bad (bad ones are really big nightmares) into little human beans' bedrooms. I was in England. Then I saw a little person peeping out of her window. She had spotted me. So I ran up to the window and grabbed her, and boy was she freaked out. I had to bring her to Giant Country. When we got there she was trying to escape. It was really getting annoying. So I gave her some of my awful food, snozzcumber. Then she started being nice to me. Her name was Sophie. She hated the other giants as well, so we set up a big, terrific plan.

So when all the giants had left to go hunting we waited a bit and then followed them.

The Meatdripper went to Spain and gobbled up lots of human beans. It was disgusting! After he went to southern Spain, we told their president. The Meatdripper was killed. One down, three to go!

The Bonecruncher went to Panama. He ate more than the last giant. We told the leader of this country as well. The Bonecruncher was killed while jumping over a hat market. One more to go!

The Gizzardgulper had went to Gabon and ate even more than the last two giants. It was horrible to watch. For the third time, we told the leader of the country a giant was in and this time the Gizzardgulper was banished from the Earth. Our job was done, and done with style!

I sadly had to leave my new best friend, Sophie, back at the orphanage in England.

My hand is tired from writing so I'll stop now. I'll write again soon.

The BFG

Charlie Rodgers (10)
Bocombra Primary School, Portadown

Sophie's First Diary Entry

(Inspired by 'The BFG' by Roald Dahl)

Dear Diary,

I have decided to start writing a diary as now it seems exciting things are going to happen after what happened last night. I'll tell you why. So, I was in the orphanage. I was still awake and I was so afraid because it was the witching hour. I couldn't sleep so I decided to look outside. I might have got punished but I didn't care. So I ducked under the curtain. I froze with fright. Something very tall and very black and very thin was in front of the Goochey's greengrocers shop.

I ran across the room and jumped into bed. I think he saw me. Suddenly, a huge hand with long pale fingers pushed aside the curtains and reached across to my bed. I screamed but the hand grabbed my duvet with me inside and withdrew his hand from the room. He galloped off and sometimes it seemed that we were flying!

That was last night. I found out that his name was the BFG. We chatted for a while, then he told me something that was ridiculous, confusing and amazing all at the same time! He told me that the other giants thought that people from Turkey taste of turkey, from Wales taste of whales, from Jersey

taste of jerseys, from Denmark taste of Labradors (?), from Labrador taste of great Danes(?), from Wellington taste of wellies, from Panama taste of hats and people from Greece taste greasy!
This afternoon I tried snozzcumbers. I do not recommend them. They taste of snot and who knows what else. I also tried frobscottle but it was delicious! The bubbles fizz all the way down! If the bubbles fizz up, it makes you burp, what happens when the bubbles fizz down? It was hilarious!
That's all from me tonight, I'll tell you about the giants tomorrow.
Sophie

Rebekah Louise Forbes (10)
Bocombra Primary School, Portadown

The Amazing Plan

(Inspired by 'The BFG' by Roald Dahl)

Dear Diary,

This day, three years ago, was the most terrifying and most fun day of my life. Let me tell you how it all began.

One night, in the old, London orphanage, I could not get to sleep. It was the Witching Hour! Suddenly, I saw a huge shadow at the window, my heart was pounding with fear!

Then the next minute a massive hand came in through the window and snatched me. I was trembling with fright.

After that, it looked like I was in a dark hole. All I could feel was me going up and down in the dark hole. Then the figure went down a slope.

Suddenly, I saw a big, tall figure. He said his name was the BFG. He said a lot of things to me, but he got his words muddled up all the time. I soon got used to it. I got to know him very well. He showed me how to dream-catch.

On the way back from the dream-catching we bumped into the giants. They were filthy! I couldn't believe how badly they treated the BFG. They threw him in the air and kicked him. I was so shocked!

When we got back to the underground house we had a plan. That day we had caught two good and five bad dreams. We decided to put the seven dreams into one bottle, then we shook them. We knew something bad would happen.

Finally, we brought the bottle to the giants. Thankfully, they were sleeping. First we poured a drop on the Meatdripper. Suddenly, he vanished in a second. Then we poured some on the Fleshlumpeater, the Bonecruncher, the Manhugger, the Childchewer, the Gizzardgulper, the Bloodbottler and the Butcher Boy. They all disappeared.

Unfortunately, we realised that the Maidmasher was still sleeping. We didn't have any of the mixture left! We ran straight back to the house and we never knew where the Maidmasher ended up.

Yours,

Sophie

Evie Mahood (10)
Bocombra Primary School, Portadown

Me And Lucy

Dear Diary,

Me and Lucy became friends in 2019 and here is how. It was a Tuesday afternoon and I was going to call for my friends, Matthew and Danny, and when I got to their door, I heard a girl's voice saying, "Are you friends with Matthew and Danny?"

I said that I was and then at the same time we both said, "Do you want to be friends?"

It was so funny because we both said yes at the same time. So we introduced ourselves and then we were walking to Lucy's house when I saw Lucy's brother and I thought he was a teenager. He is actually two years younger than us, making Nathan nine years old and that's how Lucy and me became friends. Then me and Lucy made a den called the Haunted Den and it was so creepy. I pulled a prank on Lucy and I came running out of the den, screaming! "There's a man after me!" Lucy got so scared, then I told her it was a prank. Then one year later, Lucy's dog Soda died. It was so sad. Lucy got another dog and he is called Bruno. Lucy and me call him Bruno Mars and now we are so happy being friends.

Olivia Garrett (11)

Brownlee Primary School, Lisburn

Magical Or Not?

Dear Diary,

Rose is an eleven-year-old girl who has the worst luck ever. Let me explain. So me and Rose were walking home from school. We were walking down Cooper Street when some random salesman asked her for a pound to get a teddy bear. She thought the offer was nice but refused the offer kindly. The man then said she would be cursed with an unbreakable curse. She started saying to him, "Okay mister... "

When he interrupted her saying, "Believe the curse!"

About fifteen minutes later, a dog came up and rubbed against Rose's leg. She thought it was cute so picked the dog up and gave him a hug. Little did Rose know, the dog was taking her homework. He leapt off her, running as fast as he could. I told her she could always text the teacher to tell them what had happened with her homework.

Later that evening, we decided to go to Rose's house and draw. As we were drawing, Rose's mum spilt a bit of tea on Rose's drawing. Rose and me giggled, thinking this was the curse at work. After we stopped giggling, we looked down and saw the weirdest thing. We saw her grade papers but instead of an A-, we saw an F-! Rose just stared at the papers for half an hour!

60

Then we decided to have a sleepover to make today a little better and it was a pretty normal night... until, in the middle of the night, Rose started sleep-dancing and chanting K-Pop. The next day at school, everyone was staring at Rose. It turns out that her dad accidentally posted the video of her chanting and dancing to YouTube when he thought he was just sending it to the family cloud!

Ben Cooper (10)
Brownlee Primary School, Lisburn

Sarah And Lily's Weird Adventure

27th July, 1940-2019

Dear Diary,

On a lovely sunny day in July, Lily and I decided to go to the science lab, to escape the extreme sticky, hot weather.

We arrived at the science lab and it was the most extraordinary place we'd ever seen.

In the science lab, we walked in and there was a big blue box thing. It was a time machine! We were so amazed by it.

As we looked around the room we saw all the buttons on the control panels. We looked at each other with cheeky wee smiles and we both knew what each other was thinking. Lily asked me to look inside first, then I jumped in. As the time machine door was closing, Lily jumped in and the door slammed shut. We were stuck.

All of a sudden, in that moment, noises started, lights flashed and the machine began to rise into the sky. It went faster and faster and then it just suddenly stopped.

The door opened and there was a puff of smoke. When the smoke cleared, we heard explosions and realised we were in 1940, in World War II. We looked out and saw army men running and fighting, bombs were going off, gunshots were fired rapidly. We were so scared that we hid out of sight. Then planes zoomed over us, the noise echoed all over the sky like a roar of thunder. We had to go back because we were scared to death of the time machine getting blown to smithereens. We jumped in and pushed all the buttons. The door shut and we took off. We could be stuck in this time machine forever!

Jessica Gwen Hamilton (10)

Brownlee Primary School, Lisburn

A Big Holiday

Dear Diary,

When I was going on holiday, I just could not wait. I was getting so excited. I was going to Spain for a week. But first, I had to fly to England to stay there for a week to see my little brother. I was really excited about that too. After I had stayed in England for a week, it was a two-hour drive to get to the airport.

After we waited in the line forever, we got on the plane for our two and a half hour flight to Spain. When we landed and got off the plane, I instantly felt the heat and it was a nice feeling. We got a coach to our hotel. When we got there, it was empty, apart from reception. One bad thing was that only the people in reception and some of the waiters spoke English.

The first day on holiday was very hot so we spent the day by the pool. I got to go in the deep pool but my little brother and dad had to stay in the shallow pool.

There were lots of markets nearby and I had saved some money for the holiday so I went down to the markets with my dad and Alyvia.

After we went back to the hotel to get dinner which was an amazing buffet. It had pretty much everything and afterwards we went back to our rooms. We stayed up a little late.

When we woke up we went for breakfast. It was quick because I wanted to get back to the pool. In the pool, me and my dad had some swimming races. I won one and my dad won two. Over the next five days we went to the pool, the markets, the beach and the water park.

Lochlan William Goldsborough (10)

Brownlee Primary School, Lisburn

Far From Home

Dear Diary,
Day One - Oh No!
Me and my owner were out in the forest today and something moved in the bushes. It scared me and I accidentally jumped and bucked her off. Now, I'm lost in the forest and I'm really scared. I'm going to try and get some sleep now. Night.

Dear Diary,
Day Two - Help, Where Am I?
So today, I was looking around to see if I could find my owner, but while I was looking, a man was holding something and he wrapped it around my neck. He pulled me to a trailer and now I'm stuck in the trailer and I'm really scared because I think I'm never going to see my owner again.

Dear Diary,
Day Three - Run!
I woke up this morning in the trailer and my owner was still nowhere to be seen. I started to kick the trailer door and *bang!* The trailer door just flew open. I leapt out of the trailer and I flew like the wind to get away. As I was galloping I noticed there was white stuff under me. I started to get tired after a while so I found a warm place to rest and stayed there for the night.

Dear Diary,

Day Four - Home

When I woke up, I decided to journey down the mountains. There was a river nearby so I went to take a drink. I carried on and suddenly I saw a figure in the distance. I galloped down and realised it was my owner! I was so happy!

Sienna Dalzell (11)

Brownlee Primary School, Lisburn

Peace Proms 2019

Dear Diary,

On the day of Sunday 24th February 2019, I was about to experience the most eventful, exciting day of my life. The experience was called Cross Border Orchestra of Ireland Peace Proms 2019. Anyway, let's get back to the prep for the Peace Proms 2019.

That morning, tiredly, I walked down the stairs. I had a family breakfast with my mum, dad and sister. The juice and breakfast woke me up some more. After that, I got washed and dressed while listening to the songs I would be singing. Shortly after that, my mum came and made sure I looked tidy for the concert.

We headed to Morgan's house to get the tickets and then I went to Olivia's house because her mum was taking us to the concert.

When we arrived at the SSE Arena, me and Olivia had to go and meet the choir so we could practise before the show. At Peace Proms there were lots of different medleys like the Boogie Medley, Matilda Medley, The Greatest Showman Medley, Make Some Noise, I Sing Out Peace and, last but not least, the Pop Medley.

When we did our first song, I felt less nervous and more confident. My favourite part of the show was when songs were played and everyone joined in with the soloists. Sadly, it came to an end and people started to go home. I loved the experience and hope to do something like it again.

Meadow Briggs-Hamilton (10)

Brownlee Primary School, Lisburn

Me And One Of My Best Days Ever!

Dear Diary,

In the month of November was one of the best and funniest days of my life. It was my birthday party and I had invited Lochlan who is ten and is my best friend in school, Matthew who is my best friend out of school and, finally, Darren who is also one of my best friends.

To begin with, me and my friends went to Leisure Plex and went diving. My friends, Lochlan and Darren could jump off the third board but my gut told me not to. Even when I got near it, it started to feel really scary. Just imagine a five-metre jump with four metres of water. Nine metres! So we did some diving and then we went to McDonald's, which was great. It's my favourite restaurant. Afterwards, we drove back to my house and we had a sleepover. We did an all-nighter... well we tried to. Lochlan fell asleep at 5:30am. Darren fell asleep at 5am. I fell asleep at 7am and so did Matthew.

We played Cluedo, Uno, Game of Life and we played Sherif. I got out my Nerf Guns and we took turns giving orders, it was fun. It soon went a little bit too far and we started to hide in the toilet.

We made up stories about the Bogey Man and all of us got scared, except Darren. Matthew even asked Lochlan to stand near the toilet while he was in it.

The day after, I went diving again with Matthew.

Ilja Gres (11)

Brownlee Primary School, Lisburn

The Incredible Diary Of... Snuff Suron

Dear Diary,

Yesterday was my first day at school and I'm going to tell you all about it. When somebody thinks of school, they think of teaching, books, playing in the playground... Well, not for me because the school I go to is beside a graveyard and has zombies for teachers. Miss Trunchbull is the principal and there is a devil for a cook.

8:45am Courtyard. Now this school has really weird pupils, like Buttface Billy where his face is a butt with eyes, nose and a mouth on it. And there are a lot of other weird people.

9:05am Curse Class. Curse class is a really hard subject, having to remember what to do. And most people did what they were supposed to do except from Carla Furt, because she got a potion wrong. For some reason, she brought twenty Barbie dolls which are cursed and are now alive.

12pm Secret Room. We were hiding from the Barbie dolls because they got knives and cut off a dinner lady's leg and they were singing, "Kill the humans! Tee hee hee!"

And Buttface Billy said, "Let's attack from the side!"
Then Rhubarb Rob said, "Yeah from their backside!" laughing his heart out.
The Barbie dolls heard the laughter and, although they had killed half the school, we survived.

Will Simpson (10)
Brownlee Primary School, Lisburn

The Lion Encounter

Dear Diary,

Today was a very scary day. Me and the crew decided we would go on a safari since it was our last day in Africa before we had to go back to England. So we got in our jeep and set off, with me in the passenger seat.

When we arrived, the first animal we saw was a huge giraffe, the size of the Eiffel Tower! The next animal we saw was an elephant with its calf, walking across the road. After that, we saw a huge male lion, looking fierce. It was slowly circling the jeep. Then it decided to jump straight onto my lap. I was so scared! I didn't know what to do but, worst of all, I was getting squashed. Our tour guide Jeff didn't look surprised or nervous at all. He quietly got meat out of his rucksack and threw it over the side of the jeep, making the lion jump straight off me and back onto the ground. Jeff said that every time he goes on safari, that same lion likes to jump onto the passenger's lap. That's the last time I'm sitting in any passenger seat of any jeep! I was just happy that I could breathe and I wasn't getting squashed by this 100-tonne lion any more!

So, that was my crazy day. I hope you enjoyed reading this! Speak soon!

Summer Alicia Hammond (11)

Brownlee Primary School, Lisburn

The Incredible Diary Of... Storm

Dear Diary,

I am Storm. I am writing to tell you about a very depressing event...

I was minding my own business in my dwarf-hamster cage, when I was lifted into my running ball. I could see the big people bringing my cage to the back doorstep. Oh no! They were going to clean it. I hate it when my home gets cleaned, everything gets rearranged and I have to tidy it all over again. But I do know that it smells nicer when they clean it. I ran around in my ball, knowing there was nothing I could do about it.

Later on, Ami lifted me out of my ball and carried me out of the kitchen. My cage stayed in the kitchen! She must have made a mistake, she would notice, but she didn't. She carried me to a strange new cage and sat me down. I had sniff, oh no, this was my brother Jett's cage and that meant Jett was in my cage! For a minute, all my doubts made me feel down and I felt like a nobody. I was so miserable. I looked to Ami in hope. Ami must have read my mind for she lifted me back up and within a minute, I was safe in my own familiar cage. Plus, Jett wasn't there anymore. Yippee!

Ami Stinson (11)

Brownlee Primary School, Lisburn

The Incredible Diary Of... An Idiot

Dear Diary,

I am writing in this diary to remember all the eventful experiences that have happened to me since I moved to America. But first, I should probably introduce myself. My name is Billy Bob. I moved to America and I am starting a new school tomorrow. I am not looking forward to it!
Today is school and all I need to do is be myself. Anyway, I guess I'll be writing about my day at school when I get back. See you later Diary.

Dear Diary,

Alright, I'm back from school and it was very boring... until I got up and stood up on the teacher's desk, waving my gang's flag. Yes, I run a gang and in it is only me. Anyway, to cut a long story short, I got detention. Well, my first in the new school! And now, I'm being grounded.
I forgot about this all week. I was only grounded for two days, surprisingly. Today we are going out shopping and I think I might buy some games for my PS4. Perhaps The Lego Movie 2 video game. After shopping, we are going to the IHOP.

Dexter McCormack (11)
Brownlee Primary School, Lisburn

The Incredible Diary Of... My Brother Brady

Dear Diary,

I was going swimming today! It's my five-month birthday today. Me, Mummy and Daddy were going to celebrate by swimming. I didn't even know what swimming was! We just couldn't wait! (Well I couldn't wait!)

We dropped my brother and sister off to school and we were on our way. We were there! I was so excited! What is swimming anyway?

Mummy just put me in a weird set of clothes. They kept taking photos of me and saying I'm so cute. We were going in.

Wow! It felt just like a bath but I was in clothes. It was so funny. I was in my baby floatie and we were going round and round. It was making me dizzy.

My daddy had gone! I didn't know where he went. So I started crying. My mummy told me it was okay and helped me calm down a little by taking me round again.

I was so hungry, so Mummy took me out and gave me a bottle. I didn't feel hungry anymore but I did feel sleepy. Daddy took me in a hot tub. I was so tired, I fell asleep in the hot tub.

Angel Skye Gibson (11)

Brownlee Primary School, Lisburn

The Food Fight

20th January, 2019

Dear Diary,

Today in school I was eating my school dinner with my best friends Jess and Liv, when some mashed potatoes flew over my head and onto Mrs Wilson's white top. Then some custard hit another boy and he threw some chocolate, that hit me and my friends. We all threw stuff back until everyone in the hall had joined in. Mrs Wilson and the three dinner ladies had run out of the kitchen door, just as some trifle was thrown at Mrs Duffy!
I am now in my room because I, apparently started it, but it was worth it. It was the best day ever!

21st January, 2019

Dear Diary,

Nothing really happened today. We weren't in school because every single teacher quit! Yes! I heard a rumour that Mr Elliott was last spotted at the airport getting onto a one-way flight to Australia. As for Mrs Duffy, I heard she is still at home picking mixed fruit out of her hair!

Evie McIlwrath (11)

Brownlee Primary School, Lisburn

The Incredible Diary Of... Jack The Superhero

Monday, 25th March 12:45
Dear Diary,

I am Jack. I am just an ordinary boy and I also go to Washington Primary. So I came back home from school, which was awful because Mr Craig embarrassed me by shouting at me for not having any socks on.

13:30
I am hearing some strange noises from my basement. I'll be back for a full report.

Tuesday, 26th March
I feel weird today. I told my mum and I got the day off school.

13:00
I have just discovered that I can fly around and have a super punch. Also, when I want to I can freeze people. So, the next day in school, it was weird because I could easily beat up anybody.

Dear Diary,

Friday 20:30

I have just found this diary. Guess what? I just beat a bad guy up. He had dark eyes and a cloak. He nearly got me with his magic which would have sent me to another dimension. I dodged that and I flew towards him with my fist and got him locked up. The police took him away.

Jay Leathem (11)

Brownlee Primary School, Lisburn

The Worst Day Of My Life

Dear Diary,

I had the worst day of my life. First of all, my dog broke his leg and two other things happened. Two, school was about to open. Three, someone turned off the Wi-Fi. Still trying to find out who it was.

I mean, school isn't so bad when you're chatting with your friends, outside. Instead, you have to think and do work for five hours. And when I think of high school, then my day is terrible. Think of it, homework every weekend! But then I think of myself in P1, back in the day where I only knew Oliver. Making horrible jokes that 'somehow' were funny, like when Mrs McFarland used to tell the girls to go to the bathroom every day I used to say, "Hey Oli, you should go. You're a girl too!"

Since P3, I got a best friend, Luke. I used to only play with my cousins.

Alex Andrzej Cuber (11)

Brownlee Primary School, Lisburn

The Day I Thought I Was A Superhero

Dear Diary,

Do you ever come across a day when you think you are a superhero?

Well, if you do, you're just like me.

I thought I was a superhero and it did not end well. People in my class were talking about a really cool movie, with superheroes in it. I thought it sounded cool and maybe I was a superhero. So when I got home, I dressed as a hero.

I made a pile of chairs and climbed up. When I reached the top, I got into a hero position.

Now, as we all know, superheroes fly, so I jumped off the pile of chairs. For a moment, I thought I could fly.

Next thing you know, I was lying face down on the floor! I had a big bump on my forehead. In the end, I wasn't a superhero after all.

Isla Mae Walker (11)

Brownlee Primary School, Lisburn

The War

Dear Diary,
13th November, 1913
Today I got a job as an engineer and I think that it will work out and, when I get of age, I can retire.

Dear Diary,
21st May, 1915
It's been so long since I last wrote in this diary. I can't even remember writing in it. But so much has changed since the war started. I can't believe I thought I could retire.

Dear Diary,
31st May, 1915
I joined the military and have been non-stop working and they have even been making me design new weaponry and I am working on something that I think and hope will get me promoted.

Dear Diary,
11th June, 1915
My project is finally done. I call it the VKII. It's what I call belt fed. The only problem with it is that it's really heavy and it's not really portable, but I think the officer will still be very impressed.

Dear Diary,
12th June, 1915
My invention, the VKII is now in every military camp by the officer's command. On top of that, I got a promotion!

Dear Diary,
15th June, 1915
Today was, well... terrifying. I went into the trenches for a bomb run and it wasn't successful. As I am writing this I am far behind enemy lines and I'm in a makeshift hut, just for the night.

Dear Diary,
17th June, 1915
I have been trying to study the Germans' strategy and I heard that they're planning a bomb drop on the 1st of August.

Dear Diary,
31st July, 1915
I snuck inside the bomber plane and am now inside it. I have rigged it with explosives and, if you are reading this now, it's too late for me. But for you, your family, your friends, win this war!

Joshua Parker (11)
Cairncastle Primary School, Ballygally

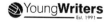

Vacation Drama

Dear Diary,

Hello, my name is Rebbecca. Last week, me and my family went on a vacation on a cruise. I adored it. Of course, my parents' favourite place was the bar.

The only bad thing was my brothers. They got their way about everything. Even in the car they got their way because Mum said we should stop somewhere for food. My brothers said KFC and I said McDonald's and who got their way? My brothers!

So on the cruise, we got a tiny cabin. There was a pull-out bed and three single beds and a double bed for my parents. I got my way this time. All my brothers were arguing about who got the pull-out bed. Although I was the only girl, I got it.

The next day, we walked to the water park. I slid down the slide but my brothers were too scared. My brothers nearly got kicked off the boat. In the karaoke room, they got hold of the microphone and started singing stupid songs and started saying, "My sister, Rebbecca is ugly!" It was really annoying.

As the day went on we went out for a family dinner. I loved it. I got a hot dog and fries. It was delicious. The dinner was going well, my brothers were behaving, but not for long. Five minutes later, my brothers screamed, "Food fight!" and they started throwing food around the room. They got in so much trouble by my parents.

The day we were due to go home came round really quickly. We were standing outside, waiting to leave, tears dripped down my face. Although my cute little brothers still made us have an amazing holiday.

Cara Noble (9)
Cairncastle Primary School, Ballygally

The Sandy Day

Dear Diary,

I was lying on the beach when I heard yelling and screaming. Straight away, I knew it was the sound of voices. It was the school that came every Monday to have a fun day out on the beach. I heard them taking off their shoes, which meant it was time to get stepped on.

All of my friends are near to the sea, which means they didn't get stepped on as much because that day they weren't allowed near the sea. I was feeling sad that day, it meant they were going to be trampling all over me because I had been washed back up onto the shore. I was going to be getting stamped on all day by children's sweaty feet. I was not going to be feeling the sun today. I was hoping I wasn't going to be the one that was going to be getting crunched between people's toes.

I was the happiest grain of sand ever because I did not get crunched between people's toes. That day at about 2pm when the school children left, I heard all the local people coming down onto the beach. I was getting picked up by a spade and getting thrown into a bucket and then getting banged on by a spade. I was being turned into a sandcastle.

I was looking at the sea and I saw the tide coming in. I got washed away in seconds and was practically drowning in the sea. I was no longer breathing and I knew in about a minute, I was going to die.

That day, I was so sick and tired as the tide was coming in and washing me and my friends away to die. I suddenly felt me drifting off, I was dead.

Lacey Moore (10)
Cairncastle Primary School, Ballygally

Christmas Day

Dear Diary,

A few weeks ago I was born in Santa's workshop. I was a very playful rabbit that loved to have fun. The fun soon ended when Santa came and took me to a separate cage from the rest of my family. He then carried me onto his sleigh. It made me feel a bit sick, but also scared because I didn't know where I was going.

The sleigh suddenly stopped and I realised it had landed. That was a relief. Santa carried me into someone's house. At first, I was nervous but it was actually a cosy and warm house.

I was sound asleep when I heard chattering and whispering from up the stairs. Then there was a *thump, thump, thump* and the door burst open and scared the life out of me. It was four children. One girl, three boys and a mum and dad. They were so excited. The girl looked at me and cupped her hands over her mouth. She stared at me. She ran straight over to me and lifted me out of my cage and cuddled me. I don't like heights so it wasn't the best feeling. Eventually, she put me back in my cage and started opening more presents. They were so loud when they opened a present that they had wanted.

Once they had opened all their presents, the girl brought me out again and took me into the kitchen. I got to play about for ages and that's when they gave me the name Ginger. Later on, I got taken in a car up to another house and played again. It was fun.

I really love my family. They play with me all the time!

Hannah Mellon (10)
Cairncastle Primary School, Ballygally

The Incredible Diary Of... Cassie Stone

23rd April, 2018
Dear Diary,
Today wasn't supposed to happen like this. Mr Helicraft wasn't supposed to fall/jump/be pushed off the school roof. And I wasn't supposed to see it. For me, life has always been normal, up to now. Well, normal enough. My purplish hair is what sets me apart from the rest. Go on, I dare you to laugh! I can hear Mia now, telling me to get back on topic. She's only jealous I was there and saw what happened and she didn't.

I saw a hooded figure back away after Mr Helicraft was pushed. I'm sure of it now. Mia is saying it has to be a teacher, no one else could have pushed an adult off a roof.

So that leaves: Mr Poylon. He is, was, Mr Helicraft's best friend. That's what I hate about dead people, the fact that everyone has to change to past tense when they say stuff about them. Mr Poylon was spotted by a shrimp (a younger person) having a disagreement with Mr Helicraft.

Miss Charena. She was seen by target practice five minutes after the murder.

Mrs Helicraft, Mr Helicraft's wife. She's completely torn over his death but Mia says we shouldn't cross her out yet.

We still have to investigate: Mrs Musialate, Mr Humfrey, Miss Bluate and Mrs Traybare, Mia's mother. Mia says she couldn't have done it but, like Mia said, if Mrs Helicraft can't be ruled out, then neither can Mrs Traybare!

Livia Alice Whelan (10)

Cairncastle Primary School, Ballygally

Eggy Problem

22nd May

Dear Diary,

This morning I woke up like always. But this time, it was a bit different because somebody knocked on my eggshell. I opened it slightly to check who it was and he immediately started chatting to me. He was saying that I was the egg and stuff I didn't understand. I told him to come in but I wasn't sure why. We had a long chat about something that was very interesting to me. That I was a super egg! I wondered why my friends had never opened their eggshells to let me in but they couldn't! The weird thing was, my new friend who told me I was super, was cheese.

23rd May

Dear Diary,

This morning I woke and the cheese knocked on my door again. We had our little chat. Cheese told me that the buttons on the side of my house (my eggshell) were to control the eggshell spaceship! Soon I was flying around like a crazy egg, then I remembered that it was Cara's birthday and I couldn't go to her party because I couldn't move out of my eggshell. But now I could go zooming around the fridge to the top.

"Cara, here I come!"

After the party, I was exhausted. I can't wait for the next adventure of Super Egg!

Beth Devaney (10)

Cairncastle Primary School, Ballygally

The Worst Day Ever!

Dear Diary,

Today was the worst day ever! Well, I mean it would be anybody's dream to be the most popular girl in the school, not to brag. But let me tell you what happened today. It started off like a normal day by putting on a full face of make-up, which took me an hour to do. Then I had to pick out my beautiful outfit which was mint-green with a cute brown belt. Now all I had to do was my hair. I curled it with my curlers. Then I was off to school and the fun started. My boyfriend was with my best friend, Claire. I went over to see what was happening and talk with Brandon. He said, "Sorry, I am so over you." and he walked away.

A few tears dropped down my cheek and my mascara was all smudged. I blocked Brendan and Claire. I told Chloe, my other best friend, and she blocked them too. Now we had to look for the third most popular girl in the school because we weren't friends with Claire anymore. We looked and looked and looked but we couldn't find anyone except this boring cheerleader. She was the least popular girl in the school so, for now, I am unpopular. That was the worst day ever.

Emily Fulton (10)

Cairncastle Primary School, Ballygally

Indoraptor's Diary

Dear Diary,

Today I was walking in the forest and I saw a wee boy jumping over a log. Obviously, I had to react so I jumped at him. Then I looked up and saw his parents. They started sprinting away but, to me, it was easy to catch them. It took me five seconds to catch them. First I bit the mum and then I gobbled up the dad.

I still wasn't pleased so I had to move closer to the park. At the time, I thought it was a good idea but now when I really think about it, it was a completely terrible idea. I don't know why I did it. When I arrived, I was hiding in the greenery. There was so much to choose from, but I had to stay focused. I decided to take it slow but it's pretty hard to go slow when you are part velociraptor. I couldn't be seen but then I saw someone holding a really delicious-looking hot dog. I couldn't resist. Just then, another man carrying a gun walked over to him. I really didn't like the look of him so I decided to go and find another meal. A while after that, I got a meal. It was In 'n' Out and was delicious. At least I got a good meal out of it.

Emelia McGeown (10)
Cairncastle Primary School, Ballygally

A Rubber's Diary

Dear Diary,

Today was the worst day of my life. First of all, Emelia (my owner and the most annoying girl ever) forgot to take me home last night so I lay on the desk, freezing all night. When she came in this morning, she kept biting me and chewing me. So then I had loads of bite marks on me.

Later on, after break, she came in and during English she kept stabbing me and taking big chunks out of me.

After lunch, she kept rubbing me on the table. She also started chopping me up and throwing me around the classroom.

Finally, it was home time but the worst wasn't over because she had her pencil case out on the bus. She was doing homework but was using a pen. I fell on the floor and rolled about halfway down the bus into some weird, wet stuff and stayed there all night, until the bus driver found me and handed me back to Emelia.

The thing is that Emelia does all this to me and she doesn't even own a pencil! It's hard being a rubber.

Tyler Campbell (11)
Cairncastle Primary School, Ballygally

The Incredible Diary Of... Cuddles (A Teddy Bear)

Dear Diary,

Today I got put on the shelf. I am so happy, I might get someone to live with. I want a nice loving family. I got sat with toys. I sat beside a crazy doll, a tractor was on the other side of me with some books. I found a blank book and named it Cuddle's Diary. I am on the high shelf so kids can get me. All day, I wrote and wrote while the doll shouted at me. The tractor had no remote control so it didn't move. A little girl came into the store. Her mum told her she could get one toy. She looked all over the store for a toy. Everyone stood still, wanting to have a new life with a new family. I wanted to get closer so I went to the bottom shelf. She looked behind her and saw me. She picked me up and ran to her mum. Her mum told her to get a book too so she picked up my diary. I am in a home now.

Ava-Grace Shaw (11)

Cairncastle Primary School, Ballygally

Diary Of Sarah The Seahorse

Dear Diary,

Today I was swiftly swimming like usual, when I swam past a seahorse who had lost something. I offered to help. She shook her head with no emotion. I was hurt. I knew something was wrong but didn't know what. I helped anyway. Then she finally told me her baby was stuck in the rocks. What was even worse was the baby had just been born. I said, "Call the dolphins or just grab her tail!" She got her and I was so happy that I had helped save someone. I jumped up and down laughing and crying tears of joy with her.

It turns out she owned a pizza restaurant. So I learned my lesson and I'm being nice to everyone now.

Katie Kirkpatrick (10)
Cairncastle Primary School, Ballygally

A Titanic Diary

Dear Diary,

I am sad to say that the Titanic is sinking and my chances of getting on a lifeboat are very, very slim. I love you all. You are all shooting stars. For my two children and my beloved wife, reach for your dreams because you will always catch them. The women and the children are boarding the lifeboats as I write. I am in the first class smoking room, having a cigarette and some whisky to warm me up because it is freezing. But I am sick of it. Carpathia 6 is trying to come but it is three hours away and Titanic is going to be at the bottom of the sea in twenty minutes. I have had some great times here on Titanic. It is freezing. I think I'm going to freeze! In a little while, I will be a dead boy down at the bottom of the Atlantic Ocean. This letter means a lot to me as I think it will to you too. Please always keep this precious letter and remember me. If you never see me again, my last words are you are all amazing in what you do.

Yours sincerely,

Lewis Nickelson

Lewis Millar Nimick (10)

Creavery Primary School, Antrim

A Titanic Diary

Dear Diary,
Show the kids this letter once you are done reading. The Titanic is sinking faster and faster, it's just a matter of time until it's a thing of the past. I may make it out alive, but at this horrifying state, I wouldn't think we have much of a chance. You and the kids at least are safe. It's horrifying around here. Tables are wobbling, chairs are tipping, drinks are falling and, of course, people are pushing others around. It's hectic. People aren't getting into lifeboats either because they all think it's a whole lot safer on Titanic!

They aren't letting anybody else onto the lifeboats though people who don't want to get on are being forced.

I keep asking myself, is everything going to be okay? People are worriedly walking around here, which makes sense but nobody will help them. Mothers and children are crying out to their fathers, brothers, any men in their families. I have anxiety to a whole other level. I feel afraid, lonely, like I have nothing, like everything has been torn away from me.

Children are screaming, "I want my father!"
It hurts to see little children like this, it's not fair!
Captain Smith isn't helping anyone either, to be
honest, I wouldn't be surprised if he was sitting
drinking somewhere, yet he is the one who caused
this.
It's very unfortunate that he doesn't care about
anything that's happening around here.
Anyway, I love you dearly, even if I don't make it
out alive, I will always be with you, even if you can't
see me.
Love you dearly,
Matthew

Daisy Thompson (10)
Creavery Primary School, Antrim

A Titanic Diary

Dear Diary,

If you get this letter, please take time to read it. The Titanic is starting to sink, your mother will hopefully get to America safely, but I won't. I will probably die tonight. I will see you again in Heaven, but it might be a couple of years. Everywhere there are people panicking and people lining up for lifeboats. They said I won't get on a lifeboat because there aren't enough.

Please tell my mother about this sad event. I should have listened to you when you told us not to go and to stay home. I have met this other man who helped a lady get into a lifeboat by holding her baby so she could get in. Then he went back to a deckchair, his name is Brian and me and him talked about our families. He is the same as me, he was on his honeymoon, his wife got into a lifeboat. He also has two girls at home.

They aren't letting men in because it is women and children first. I can hear children crying because they have to say goodbye. Men's wives are worried about what's going to happen. There are signs of sadness, fear and loneliness.

The thing that I am so mad about is that Captain Smith isn't helping anyone!
I love you. I will be with you and I will watch you from Heaven when I die. Love you lots.
Your sincerely,
John

Lea Williamson (11)
Creavery Primary School, Antrim

A Titanic Diary

Dear Diary,

Not very much time to explain, so all I can say is you will be able to understand when Da lets you read the paper in a couple of days. I wish I could say I'm having a good time at the moment, but I'm not. Probably because my body will be lying at the bottom of the Atlantic Ocean in a few hours, although I have heard that dying is rather peaceful, just like falling asleep.

Tell Mother and Father that I am fine but that I won't be coming home. I also have to say, and I mean this with all my heart, that you have been the best sibling possible. Sorry that I can't send you some sneaky sample food, but if I put it in my diary, it would ruin it. I do hope that Da spoils you lots more now, with fancy new dresses, more allowance money and much more chocolate.

I have had the best time in the world on the beautiful RMS Titanic. I have heard so many people saying, "I love you more than anything." So I am saying the same.

Your sister,

Grace Sweden

Hannah Quinn (11)

Creavery Primary School, Antrim

A Titanic Diary

Dear Diary,

I am writing to tell you that I love you so much. But I don't think I am going to make it. The Titanic is sinking fast. They are putting women and children on lifeboats first. There was this one gentleman that was kind enough to take the time to help a woman and her baby onto the lifeboat. They have shut the gate on third class down on the deck. They won't let them up in case they push through the crowd. I am worried that I am not going to survive and then I will never see the family ever again. I am so frustrated that Captain John Smith is not out here. He should be out here comforting people, making them feel safe. I met a nice gentleman, he was called Mason Port. He said, "Do you want to go for a drink with me and my friends?"

I said no because I wanted to help the people out on deck. Some of the people on the deck have a look of fear and sadness on their faces. Tell my wife and children that I love them.

Yours sincerely,

Justin

Emily Adair (11)
Creavery Primary School, Antrim

A Titanic Diary

Dear Diary,

I am in such a bad situation. The Titanic is sinking and I might not make it back home, but just remember that I love you so, so much. I am so, so sorry that I can't make it back, but it's just one of those things. It is happening to other folk as well, but it's my family I am writing to because I love you all so, so much. I am doing this just for you so that I could get you and our children on a lifeboat. I can't believe this is really happening to me, but I am doing it for you. Please, please remember me and this moment and please, please keep yourself safe and all three of our children. It will be so hard but you never know, I could make it, but we're not quite sure. I'm sorry to have to go but the ship has broken in half. I love you so much. I am crying a lot. Love you and our children so, so much. Bye. I'll see you in Heaven.

Yours sincerely,

Jeff

Phoebe Grace Caldwell (10)

Creavery Primary School, Antrim

A Titanic Diary

Dear Diary,

As you know, I'm on a trip of a lifetime, but just about two hours ago, I was told the bad news that the boat was going down. They are letting ladies and children onto the lifeboats first. I also heard Mr Andrews say there won't be enough lifeboats for all of the passengers. I have seen some weird things on this ship. For example, there was a family with a baby, but it was like the baby could see someone and wanted to play with them. I felt like crying when I was on the deck. I heard a little girl shouting, "Can I please get on a lifeboat?"

I have seen lots of emotions too. Happy, sad, frightened and lots more. I don't think I will make it. I just want to say, I love you with all my heart. I'm looking forward to seeing you in Heaven.

With love,

James McKey

Louise Hill (10)
Creavery Primary School, Antrim

A Titanic Diary

Dear Diary,

I am writing to say I love you. The Titanic is sinking and I don't think I will make it to see you. Meanwhile, my wife and children are on a lifeboat on the way to dry land and they might make it to see you. I will try and get on a lifeboat. However, women and children get on first. I can't see Captain Smith. There are hundreds of women and children waiting for a lifeboat, and there is only five boats left. We are out on the Atlantic Ocean and there are no boats near us. As time goes on, half of the boat has been taken out by the iceberg. The food and the boat is lovely but I am so sad this happened, and I am so thankful Mary and the children got on a lifeboat. I wish I could see you, you are beautiful and I love being near you.
From Spencer, your brother.

Megan Bremner (10)
Creavery Primary School, Antrim

A Titanic Diary

Dear Diary,

I don't think I'm going to make it so I want you to have this letter so you will always remember me and I want you to know that I love you through the good times and the bad. You work hard at school and work and last of all, I want you to know that I will always watch you from above. It looks like people are really scared and there are children shouting for their parents and it's really cold. The boat isn't horizontal! And the deck is packed, despite all the panic there was a first class gentleman who helped a lady who didn't trust anyone. She trusted him so he held her baby while she got into the lifeboat and then handed the baby to her. I hope you have a good life in America and hope to meet you in Heaven.

Yours sincerely,

Bob Gilrow

Ben Alexander McCosh (11)

Creavery Primary School, Antrim

Titanic Diary

Dear Diary,

As you know, I am on the Titanic and it hit an iceberg. It has started to sink and I am in second class. Ladies and children are getting on the lifeboats first but there are only sixteen lifeboats. I might not make it onto one. There are people and children everywhere.

"Help me, Mother!" That was the cry of a child rushing past me.

People are wondering why there is a queue. At the top of the queue, the gate is locked! Only first class are going on the lifeboats!

I am on deck now and I have helped a lady with her baby. She got on the lifeboat and I passed her baby to her. All I can hear is adults and children crying and shouting. My room is flooding and I am looking forward to seeing you in Heaven.
Love you.
Love from Josh.

Maggie Jayne Ellis (10)
Creavery Primary School, Antrim

The Death Of The Titanic

Dear Diary,

My love, Fiona Stop You were the most beautiful, attractive and marvellous wife I could have ever asked for Stop I love every single part of you, especially your eyes that shone like diamonds Stop I won't see them anytime soon Stop I won't make it to New York for sure Stop we have hit an iceberg and it's not likely I will live Stop I can hear children screaming and I can see crowds upon crowds of people on deck Stop Please don't worry, I will be okay Stop This will be an emotional time for you, but you are a strong, independent woman Stop I have put Amy in a lifeboat Stop She will arrive in New York soon Stop I told her she will see you soon Stop She misses you dearly Stop I will meet you in Heaven. Stop

Your husband,

James Dormo

Willow Dawson (11)

Creavery Primary School, Antrim

A Titanic Diary

Dear Diary,

Thank you Chelsea for all your help over these past few years. Tell Jeffy I love him, have a good life, get a job and a girlfriend. Tell Bobby I love him. I hope you survive and have a good life in America, get a house to live in and get a good job. At the minute, I am sitting on a deckchair, sad, lonely, worried and patient. I can hear an echo of, "Help me, please help me!"

I can see a man helping a lady on a lifeboat with a baby. I can smell the fear with people worrying and I can feel the ocean breeze blowing through my hair. I don't know if I will survive or not on the Titanic. I wanted to talk with Captain Smith about the iceberg, but he is nowhere to be seen.

Love you. Bye.

Yours sincerely,

William McAllister

Samuel Craig (11)

Creavery Primary School, Antrim

A Titanic Diary

Dear Diary,

I am writing to tell you that I might not make it home. However, I have started off well and had a lovely journey meeting new people. As time has gone by we were going to the bottom of the deep, blue sea. But I have discovered that I was a hero. There was a lovely lady called Rachel. She was struggling to get on a lifeboat with her child called Thomas. I helped her by taking Thomas off her and let her get on and then I passed Thomas to her. Then I went back and sat on a deckchair. You see, it was women and children first allowed on the lifeboats. Everybody called me, Lucas Millar, a hero. So I am sad to have to tell you that me, the Titanic and friends are going to the bottom of the deep, blue sea.

Yours sincerely,

Lucas Millar

Lucas Millar (11)

Creavery Primary School, Antrim

RMS Titanic Diary

Sister Bethan,

Not very much time to write this, but all I have to say is, I love you with all my heart, because I might not make it. Everyone is running about screaming, shouting and cursing. Half of the people are not getting onto the lifeboats and people are jumping off the boat. I saw a man holding a woman's baby until she got on the lifeboat, it made me heartbroken to see a man do that because a lot of people are only bothering about themselves. He was a miracle, lovely man. I have to say bye now, before I drown writing this letter.

Yours sincerely,

Sister Alexa

Gracie Alexa Rose Doran (11)
Creavery Primary School, Antrim

The Incredible Diary Of... Cecil!

Dear Diary,

As I trotted through the forest on a sunny spring morning, I encountered a strange pink glowing light in a tree. I crept towards it and the light changed to yellow, then green, red, blue, orange, purple. It was a magnificent sight. The colourful illusion got bigger, bigger, bigger until I was staring at a multicoloured... what was it? A portal? Well, there was only one way to find out... "Oof!" Oops! I jumped too low. *Whoosh!* It was a portal! I wondered where it would take me - a tropical island? A forest ruled by dinosaurs? A world of talking vegetables? Unfortunately, it was the second thought - a land covered in dinosaurs. Typical. Just typical.

Suddenly, the ground shook. *Boom!* Was it a-*Boom!* There it was again! *Boom!* Hold on! I'd seen this happen in movies before. It usually meant... that the dinosaur... was behind them! I turned around, shaking. I was right! "Argh!" I ran up a tree, although it wasn't a tree, it was a cactus. So I ran again with loads of prickles on my fur. I noticed a familiar light. The portal! Yes! I leapt through. Phew! What a day!

Claire McClements (10)

Ebrington Primary School, Londonderry

The Incredible Diary Of... A Champions League Winner

An extract

14th April

Dear Diary,

It's the day after the semi-final of the Champions League, we progressed to the final, the unbelievable has happened. It's what every footballer wants to achieve, to get to a big final. Six weeks later and we could be sitting on top of the world.

16th April

Dear Diary,

Training day. Meeting up with the boys and getting ready for the next match. Training goes well but five minutes from the end, in a five versus five, I clash heads with one of my teammates. I'm down, I'm scared, there's so much pain and then the emotions. All I can think about is, will I make the final? The physios help me off, and I'm away for a scan to check out the damage. The swelling is down and I'm not too bad, but I haven't heard anything about the scan.

The doctor and the physios return. They have diagnosed a fractured eye socket and mild concussion. My first thought is that it's six weeks to the final... Am I going to make it? The doctor gives me a moment to gather my thoughts. He tells me I must not play sports for at least four weeks. Again, the emotions take over. I may have to miss the game of my life!

30th April
Dear Diary,
It's two weeks since the incident. I am very low and my mood isn't good. I've been in the gym every day, keeping up my fitness. I feel good and the physios have prescribed the use of a protective headguard when I start back, but I'm worried I won't get my place back.

14th May
Dear Diary,
First day back of training, the league season is over and all we have left is the final. Will I be able to do enough to get my place back in the team? Training goes well, my energy levels are high and I feel I've really shown that I'm ready.

29th May
Dear Diary,
The day before the final game, today we hear who
is on the team.
Yes! I'm in!

James Smallwoods (10)
Ebrington Primary School, Londonderry

Max's Trip To Space

Dear Diary,

My name is Max and I am going to space with my uncle in an hour so I will write when I am on my way. Right now, I'm in the rocket and I'm excited and a bit nervous. The rocket is huge and full of fun games. I've now arrived in space and I'm so excited. Me and my uncle George think we've discovered a new planet. We are going to go and explore this new planet right now. We've now landed on the planet and I'm overwhelmed with happiness. This planet is full of weird alien-looking people all around three feet tall. After talking to these people we have worked out that everyone is called Sarah and there is a huge fight over who is the real Sarah. It is around 6:30pm and we are really hungry, so the Sarahs offer us dinner.

For dinner we are having some weird, gloopy, rainbow mush, which was actually really nice. Now we are on our way home and we're going to go meet up with some scientists to tell them about the planet we've discovered. Guess what? My uncle said, if we get to the name the planet, I can choose the name! I have thought of a name and I think I am going to name the planet Oobla.

Hollie Thomas (11)
Ebrington Primary School, Londonderry

The Birthday

Dear Diary,

It is my birthday tomorrow and my parents say they have a big surprise for me. I am extremely excited. I've already had my birthday party where all my friends and family came to Lenamore Stables for a pony party. We played lots of games like 'What's the Time Mr Wolf?' and also got to groom the horses.

Afterwards, we went to the party room where we played music and had lots of party food. My cake was in the shape of a horse's head and tasted amazing. Then it was time to open my presents from my friends and family. I got a horse lead rope, a saddle, stirrups, bridle, a saddle pad, a whip and a helmet.

It was time for everyone to go home. I was so tired after all the excitement. I had some supper and am going to bed.

Dear Diary

I've just woken up. Yay! Today is my birthday and the day I get a surprise! I rushed downstairs and Mum told me to eat my breakfast and get changed into my horse riding stuff and grab all my new horse stuff that I got for my birthday. We all jumped into the car and went to Lenamore Stables.

I got out of the car at the stable and saw a sign saying *Happy Birthday Isabella*. My mum covered my eyes and took me to a stable. When she took her hands away, there was my surprise. A beautiful brown horse with a plaited mane and a pink bow was standing in front of me.

"Happy birthday Isabella!" my mum said. "She is your surprise!"

I was so excited, I hugged my mum tight. I got Angel all sorted and we went to the paddock. We did some small jumps and some trotting. After a few hours it was time to go home. I didn't want to leave Angel but Mum said we could come back tomorrow. This has been the best birthday ever!

Rihanna Borland (11)

Ebrington Primary School, Londonderry

The Incredible Diary Of... Nat The Robot

Dear Diary,

The other day, something really strange happened. My name is Nat. I live on Mars and I love it here. So, anyway, I was cleaning my room and under the bed I found a small metal disc. It was purple and dusty, so I blew off the dust. Then all of a sudden, a portal opened and sucked me inside! I found myself in a strange room with paper stacks which had words in them, and I'm pretty sure humans call them books. I opened the door and everything was so... strange and different! I took a step forward but I had to go back quickly because there was something wet, which would harm me a lot because I'm a robot. I was about to go around the wet thing when a small hand touched my shoulder. It was a tiny human.

"Hi," she said. "My name is Emily. What's yours? Cool costume by the way!"

I told her my name was Nat and it wasn't a costume, but that didn't put her off.

"Okay then Nat. Wanna play a game?" she asked me.

"No, wait! Yes! Let's play find the purple metal disc!" I replied.

"You mean this?" she said, holding it up.

"Yes!" I cried. Then she yelled something like, "Can't catch me!" and ran away.

"Stop!" I yelled, but she didn't listen. I chased after her, but there were so many wet things I couldn't because it was too risky. I eventually caught up with her and she said I could have the disc back, I reopened the portal, gave Emily a quick hug, and jumped in. I was home! I never told anyone about what happened because they wouldn't believe me, but I know it happened. I often think of Emily and if I should visit her.

Catherine Campbell (10)

Ebrington Primary School, Londonderry

Miracle At Eglington Horse Show

Dear Diary,

Last week I entered my horse (Patch) into the Eglington Horse Show and I was really excited. But now that a week has past, I'm really nervous because my horse won't go over the jump and tomorrow is the show. So, now before it gets dark, I'm going to practise as much as possible. Today is the day of the horse show and I am super nervous now.

Around three days before I said to my dad, "I think I'm going to back out of the competition," but my dad believes in miracles so he thought a miracle would happen or something like that.

I just got dressed for the horse show and when I got there, I saw a practice arena. I decided to practise one more time, really quickly, because I'm going first. I tried to practise going over the jump, just no luck. He just wouldn't go over the jump. I got in line with the other competitors and about five minutes after the announcer had finished talking, I was called out.

The sweat was running down me like pouring rain, I was so nervous, but then I remembered my mum had given me a shamrock necklace before she died. Before me and my horse went out to the jumping course, I told him to not be scared of the

126

jump, to just do it. It took me two minutes to complete the course and I was so happy and surprised for two reasons. 1- Patch went over the jump and made a clear round. 2 - Most of the other competitors finished in three minutes.

I waited another five minutes for the announcer to announce the winner and they said I was first! But I was so nervous that I didn't actually hear them. I was so happy and I told Patch I would give him five carrots.

Bonnie McQue (11)
Ebrington Primary School, Londonderry

The Incredible Diary Of... Wheelz!

Dear Diary,

I woke up this morning to find my mum sitting on my bed. Today is my birthday. I am eight years old. The only thing wrong with today is I had to go to hospital. I go to hospital to get tests done a lot and it can be very boring.

"Sky," said Mum, "You have to get up for the hospital, and by the way, happy birthday. Sky, you're going to have a wonderful day!"

Hmmm. I wondered what Mum could mean. Maybe she was planning a party...

After my test at the hospital, Mum said, "Sky, now for your surprise!"

Wow! I wondered as I got into my wheelchair. By the way, it's why my friends call me Wheelz. I think it's a cool nickname. Mum put me and my chair in the car and started driving.

"Where are we going?" I asked.

"You will see soon."

We arrived soon after at this big house in the country.

"Happy birthday Sky! This is your present."

I thought to myself, *my present is a big house*? But, just then I saw a horse out of the corner of my eye. It was white, with gold, shiny hair.

Just then, I realised my mum got me a pony! I felt super happy, amazed and all the sad feelings I had about being sick went away. Just then, the horse ran through the gates like lightning and I thought I would never see her again.

Half an hour passed and my mum stopped me crying. "Sky," she said, "look quickly!"

I looked to see Alexa, my sister, and what I know to be my pony, Angel, walking towards the car. This was the best birthday ever!

I have to go now because my mum has told me to go to sleep!

Brooke Margaret Bridget Kerr (10)

Ebrington Primary School, Londonderry

The Escape Of Silly Sausage

Dear Diary,

Today I was playing in my pack with my brothers. Mum said to be careful, but it was too late. I fell out of my packet and onto the shop floor. I tried to climb back onto the shelf but I kept falling off.

After three attempts I fell so hard that I rolled along the floor. That's when a man picked me up and took me! I tried calling for help, but it was no use. Nobody could hear me.

Next thing I knew, I was in a restaurant! I was so lonely. I missed my family.

After a while, the man came back. There were lots of people there. One of the men shouted, "Sausage supper!"

I knew I had to escape, but before I could, I was grabbed and put into a pan with oil. It was really slippery. I rolled about trying to escape and after a few tries, I fell out of the pan and made a run for it. The man was shouting, "Come back here!"

He tried to grab me but, thanks to the oil, I slipped out of his hands and fell onto the floor. Every time I tried to run, I slipped and fell and was almost stood on.

Finally, I found an open door and snuck outside. Thankfully, the supermarket was beside the restaurant. I made a run for it but a dog came running for me. I tripped over and fell into a bush. The dog couldn't find me. Once the dog was gone. I made a run for the supermarket door.

When I got into the supermarket, the floor was really slippery. I tried to run but slipped and skidded along. Finally, I stopped, but bumped my head on the shelf. Mum saw me and my family made a sausage chain to help me back up. I was so happy to see my family again.

I will never play in the packet again.

Tristyn Nathan Taggart (9)

Ebrington Primary School, Londonderry

Mischief

An extract

Monday, 15th May

Dear Diary,

Today was the worst day ever! I got humiliated in front of the whole class because stupid Lucas put a bucket of water on the door so when I went into class I got soaking wet!! I absolutely despise Lucas because he's always pulling stupid pranks on me. Argh! I've looked on the Internet for any decent pranks but they're all babyish so I've decided to do a bunch of different pranks on him. He he he... Watch out Lucas!

Okay, I've got a bunch of pranks written down. Like filling his glue with powder at the bottom and a thin layer of glue at the top. Lucas always has a jam bun for lunch. Yuck! So I'll sneakily fill it with ketchup when he goes for football practice. And this is the most evil out of them all. Mwahahahaha! I will put a horn on his chair and when he sits down it will go off and... I will also put a whoopee cushion on his chair as well. So it goes off at the same time. Mwahahahahaha!

Tuesday, 16th May

Dear Diary

Today is the day! I'm getting all the pranks ready now. I've got to go to school now but I'll write all the information after school.

Dear Diary

This is what today went like: I got to school early to set everything up. When everyone else got into school, Lucas tried to use his glue, but little did he know I had put flour at the bottom of it and it all fell out onto his work. Ha ha! Oh wait, I forgot the chair prank. He sat down on the chair and the horn went off and scared him, then the whoopee cushion went off and everyone burst out laughing.

Riley Kennedy (10)
Ebrington Primary School, Londonderry

Abbie's Dream

Dear Diary,

My name is Abbie O'Connell. I am a sixteen-year-old student. I have a big sister called Freya that I don't really see that much. I don't really have many friends at school. I always have my big sister by my side... but she left for university. I really miss her. I'm going to audition for X Factor in a week, which is very exciting. My family have always supported me. My parents have always said, "Never give up on your dreams!"

My grandmother always used to come to my school concerts. My music teacher always told me I was a good singer, which gave me the confidence to pursue my dreams.

Monday

Dear Diary,

It's the start of a new week and five more days to go until the audition which is exciting, but I'm really nervous. I have choir practice every day this week, which will hopefully help my voice for Saturday.

Wednesday

Dear Diary

Yesterday, I told people I was auditioning for X Factor. They didn't believe me. One of the girls, called Summer, was really nice to me. She said I should definitely win because I have a beautiful voice.

Saturday

Dear Diary

The day has finally come. I have been waiting for this day since I was a little girl. Most of my family members are coming. I wish Freya could see me perform.

My new friend, Summer said she could come with me. We are getting a train from our home in Manchester, to London. I won't be able to write anymore til tomorrow. Fingers crossed.

Holly Nicole Clifford (11)

Ebrington Primary School, Londonderry

Welcome To My World

Dear Diary,

Hi, I'm Savannah. I'm 11 years old with two sisters, Sara who is younger than me and Millie who is older than me.

Today was our first day at a new school. I moved from Australia to England. At the start of today, I had to get up super early, while my older sister was relaxing in her bed. She starts school later than me. My younger sister, Sara, was already making her lunch for the day. So then I had an hour to get ready.

I walked to school because my mum thought it would super good for me because I'm always on my phone. When I got to the school gates, it was very scary. There was this man (who I learnt later was the principal) giving out letters. I took one and it was all about the school and a map of the school. When I got into my first class, there were these really nice girls who introduced themselves and I learnt that two of the five girls had younger, annoying sisters.

At break time, the group of girls wanted to hang out with me and showed me who was who and who not to talk to. I really like this guy called Purri, he's so cute and really nice to me.

Lunchtime then rolled around and nearly everyone wanted to talk to me and ask me questions. I felt like a movie star or something. Even Purri wanted to talk to me. By the end of the day I had almost everyone's number. I practically ran home in excitement to tell my mum, and I think Millie was jealous.

Well, goodnight Diary. Talk to you tomorrow.

Sienna Faye Campbell (11)

Ebrington Primary School, Londonderry

The Incredible Diary Of... Virgil van Dijk

Dear Diary,

I attended training tonight with my teammates. My training session was tough but I got through it. We were training for five hours with breaks in-between. The reason we train hard is because we want to win the title over Manchester City. The big match is on tomorrow and it's taking place at Anfield football stadium. My teammates and I are so fit and ready for tomorrow's massive game.

Dear Diary,

I woke up fresh this morning as it's match day. Last night, I dreamt that we won the title. I felt amazing. As the match approached, the crowd started to gather. The atmosphere was electric and I started to get excited. When all the players arrived in the changing room, our manager, Jurgen Klopp, gave us a team talk to remember. As we walked down the tunnel, we heard the crowd shouting, "Come on Liverpool!"

As the match kicked off, we went 0-1 down in the first five minutes. As half time was approaching, City were on the counter-attack.

I made a silly foul and the referee called Mike Dean gave a penalty to City. Agüero scored to make it 0-2 at half-time. The second half began and we pulled one back, Mané scored.
The 90th minute up popped Lovren with a volley to make it 2-2. Up came the board with four minutes. Three minutes have passed and we got a corner. Everyone came up, the ball floated in, *bang*, I scored the winner. What a feeling! Liverpool won the title!

Dylan McPoyle (11)
Ebrington Primary School, Londonderry

The Incredible Diary Of... Harry Kane

Dear Diary,

My radio alarm goes off at 7:00. I lie and listen to the news headlines, waiting for the sports news to hear what they have to say after our victory in the North London Derby yesterday.

After breakfast, I drive to the training ground, picking up the newspapers on the way to read the sports headlines when I'm getting ready for training.

Training starts at 10:00 and lasts for two hours. Because yesterday's match was a late kick-off, today's training will be light.

From 12:00 to 13:00 we watch a short video of the match yesterday. Maurice and the other staff point out the good and bad points of our play in the game.

At 14:00 we have a light lunch, prepared by the chef at the training ground. I would normally have pasta with chicken.

At 14:30, the squad sit down to watch videos of Liverpool, our opponents on Wednesday night. This is to see what their strengths and weaknesses are. we also discuss tactics for the match on Wednesday night.

At 16:00 we shower and get dressed and drive home. It is now family time with my partner, Katie and children, Ivy Jane and baby Vivienne. After the children go to bed, I take Brady and Wilson, my two Labradors, for a walk on the common.

19:30 we sit down to have our evening meal prepped by Katie. After the meal we watch a film on television.

22:30. Off to bed to get plenty of rest for another day's training at Enfield Training Centre.

Christian Patterson (11)

Ebrington Primary School, Londonderry

The Incredible Diary Of... A Football Player

Dear Diary,

Today was the day I made my debut for Manchester City. I was feeling a mix of nerves and excitement. I woke up at 6:30am to get my breakfast before I left my spectacular house.

I drove down to the training grounds to catch the spacious, fancy bus to today's opposition, West Ham United. It took two hours to get there so we arrived at 8:30am. I went into the changing rooms to get changed into a training kit. Once I got into the kit, I came to get a quick training session.

After about 45 minutes, I ran back in the changing room to get ready for the match as the manager announced the starting line up. Sadly, I was on the bench to start off with. I was totally expecting it but as long as I get some playing time.

Finally, the match started and I think we had our strongest team out there. It was the 50th minute and no one had scored and there were still forty minutes left.

Eventually, the manager decided to bring me on as a left wing. I know I was only on for fifteen minutes, but I did something you might not believe. It was a corner and the ball fell to my feet, I didn't know whether to pass or shoot but of course, I decided to shoot.

I struck the ball as hard as I could with my laces and, all of a sudden, the ball hit the back of the net and all of the fans started to scream and cheer.

This day has to be one of the best days of my life.

Ben Campbell Haslett (11)
Ebrington Primary School, Londonderry

The Incredible Diary Of... Adabelle's Messy Puppy

Dear Diary,

Today is my birthday and I really wanted a new science kit. In most of my cards there was money because there was no present.

Time to go downstairs. Weirdly, there weren't any annoying brothers in the room. Hmmm. (I have two brothers, Michael and David.) Usually, I am the first one up anyway.

Yes, my first present was a science kit. Yay! Strangely, my dad handed me a dog bone. He told me to open Mike's door. As I opened the door, you'll never guess, but there was... a dog! It was so cute. It had brown fur and brown eyes, with a white stripe on its chest. I'm going to take her on a walk (I called her Libby), see you tomorrow.

Dear Diary

Yesterday was so fun. I was going to go on a walk, but the dog didn't have a lead or harness. I bought some, well, picked some out. So now I can take her out for a walk. She got to sleep in my room last night too! She started off sleeping downstairs in her crate but kept whining so she settled on my bed.

Mum probably took her downstairs in the middle of the night because when I woke up, she wasn't there. Mum brought her into me when I woke up. When I went downstairs for breakfast, I realised that Libby had ripped up her lovely, fluffy, new bed. Now I've got to go and tell my mum. I have told Libby off and she looks so sad! Talk to you next time.

Anna Curtis (11)
Ebrington Primary School, Londonderry

The Lost Puppy

Dear Diary,

You will never guess what happened to me this week. My dog, Fluffy, got lost. I was getting money from the bank and Fluffy was in the park. He ran away because he smelt a bone. When I got back from the bank, he wasn't there. I was so sad. I went home and made posters to put on trees and lamp posts.

That night, I went everywhere looking for Fluffy but there was no sign of him. I decided to go back home and get some rest to get up early the next morning to look for Fluffy. I couldn't sleep that night because I was worried about Fluffy.

The next day, I woke up so early to look for Fluffy but still no sign! I kept looking, I couldn't stop. Fluffy was my best friend so I kept looking. I looked over at a lamp post and there was a sign that said there was going to be a theme park tomorrow. I thought that would be a great idea to go and look for Fluffy. It was getting dark so I went back home and went to bed to get some rest. I still couldn't sleep, so I kept trying.

The next day I got up early to go to the theme park. I arrived and started looking for Fluffy.

I spotted something over near the photo booth. It had black spots, a purple collar and a name tag that said Fluffy. I was ecstatic to see him! I was so happy, I cried. I took Fluffy and lifted him up in my arms and hugged him. I squeezed him really tight.

Armani Mitchell (9)

Ebrington Primary School, Londonderry

The Crazy Queen Bee

Dear Diary,

Hi, I'm Tara. The alarm clock went off, time to get up for school to do work for a whole six hours. My little sister's the luckiest person in the world because she gets to go to nursery all day and sing songs, draw pictures, play and sleep. In my opinion, I wish I could be her.

Well, I guess, off to school. We did literacy and more literacy and numeracy and more numeracy. Finally, school was over. Time to go home. But first we needed to pick up my little sister. Then we had to go and get milk from the shop. Then we had to go to Granny's and finally, we got to go home.

I did my homework first, ten divided by twelve, then twelve divided by ten and so on. Then we had our dinner and it was 6pm.

After that I went to my bedroom. I opened the window because it was roasting. A piece of paper flew in the window. Pretty strange right? It said, 'This will change your life!'

"Wait! What will change my life?" I said.

All of a sudden, a bee flew into my bedroom and it talked! Weird right? It told me that I would be a superhero and save Paris. It gave me a necklace. I put it on and something crazy happened.

148

Suddenly, I was yellow with black stripes. I was Queen Bee. Let's go save the world and fight crazy villains.

Eloise Catherine White (9)

Ebrington Primary School, Londonderry

The Incredible Diary Of... My Mum

Dear Diary,

On Tuesday morning, I get up at 7am and get ready for work. I then get Ben and Sophie up and dressed for school. Then I come downstairs and get Ben and Sophie's breakfast ready.

While Ben and Sophie are having breakfast, I make sure that their packed lunches or dinner money is in their school bags and also their break snack. I then get Ben and Sophie's hair done and our coats on and then I finish getting myself ready for work. After the kids go to school, I walk to my friend's house to wait for my lift to work. I work with people with learning disabilities. While at work, I have to get my clients tea and toast when they come in, look after their personal care, take them on outings either for lunch or a cafe. I love the job I do as it makes me feel happy at the end of the day. I feel like I have made a difference to my clients' lives.

I then come home from work and I look after my disabled sister for a couple of hours. I also help Ben and Sophie with their homework and prepare the dinner for the family.

I then get Ben and Sophie ready to go to karate and personal training. I get ready to go to zumba with my friend, no matter how tired I am.
When I come back from zumba, I get the kids' supper and get them ready for bed.

Ben McKnight (10)
Ebrington Primary School, Londonderry

The Incredible Diary Of... Steven Gerrard

Dear Diary,

As I woke up this morning, I was feeling very excited and nervous. This was our big day. We played Athletico Madrid in the final of the Champions League at Wembley Stadium.

After breakfast with my family, I drove to Anfield to meet up with the rest of my team. Our manager, Jurgen Klopp, gave us a stern team talk. The team coach arrived and we travelled down to Wembley Stadium. I warmed up with the rest of the team. The time had come, the Champions League Final. I was buzzing. We were playing for twenty minutes when Athletico Madrid made a quick break and scored. I was devastated. At half-time, the score was one-nil. The manager told us what he expected from us in the second half. Out to the pitch we went, within ten minutes Robbie Fowler scored and levelled the match. I was elated. We had this within our grasp.

With just four minutes of play left Riise played a long ball to me and I ran for goal. There was no one in front of me, and I blasted right past the keeper. We were two-one up and there was only one minute left.

We played our hearts out until the final whistle. We were the new European champions. We had done it!

So, dear Diary, this was the best day of my life.

Jason Patterson (11)
Ebrington Primary School, Londonderry

The Incredible Diary Of... The Mermaid Molly

Dear Diary,

Today I found a strange greenish blueish fish of some sort. It had a hard shell and its head looked a bit funny. I showed it to my parents who told me it was a turtle.

"A turtle?" I said. "What's that?"

"Well, it's a funny-looking thing that you used to see way back, like nine million years ago," said my dad.

"Dad, no more history. I am sure the no one wants to hear about nine million years ago!" I said.

Later I was in my room, doing some maths, like 242=fish and my mermaiden history when suddenly, there was a knock on my door. It was my dad. Groan! He shouted at me for getting a mer3 on my test, which is a good grade (not). He was so mad, I wasn't allowed on my merpad for a week. (3 days.)

Then my mum came in, more bad news. My sister might as well come in and shout at me for something! My mum threw the turtle (Turtlecious) in the mercook. "He'll be a tasty dinner for tonight!" she said.

I got a new seashell and that was about it so I'll stop writing now. Bye.

Amelia Doherty (10)
Ebrington Primary School, Londonderry

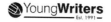

The Incredible Diary Of...

Dear Diary,

It's me, Chewbacca, back again to write about what happened to me when I was defending my home planet, Kashyyyk.

The Republic turned on us and captured me and half of my fellow Wookiees. The Republic transported me to a different planet and made me stay locked in a cell. I thought I would never return home. I sat in my cell for fifty years, telling myself to have faith that rescue was coming.

One day, a gate opened. I thought I was going to be saved by my fellow Wookiees, but instead, it was a human man. I felt scared. I thought he was going to hurt me, but instead, he saves my life. His name was Han Solo and together we make a pact that we will escape. We have planned our escape. I found some rope. Han tied it round me and the cell bars and he told me to pull with all my strength. I broke the bars and we found a spaceship. I felt so happy that finally I would be going home. Me and Han Solo escaped the Republic, which was now called the Empire.

I made it back to my home planet after fifty years. I owe my life to Han Solo, my best friend.

Brandon Gleed (11)

Ebrington Primary School, Londonderry

156

Harry Potter And The Attack

Dear Diary,

Hi, my name is Harry Potter. I am fifteen years old and I attend Hogwarts School of Witchcraft and Wizardry. My best friends are Hermione Granger and Ron Weasley and I have a pet owl called Hedwig. A wizard called Voldemort killed my parents. However, I survived and that has made me very well known in the wizarding world. Voldemort has attacked me while I have been at Hogwarts, but I have always been very lucky and got away with a few cuts and bruises. This time, I didn't get away so easily. I was in Godric's Hollow and a black cloud of smoke came through the door. I felt so frightened, but I knew I had to save everyone. He had already killed Cedric Diggory and I wasn't letting him kill anyone else. I told everyone to run and everyone tried to, but I didn't know if they got out because the cloud vanished and Voldemort turned into a snake. He bit my leg and my arm, but I kept fighting and I used my wand with the spell, *Incendio*, which started a fire and Voldemort went up in smoke.

This was the end of Voldemort for now...

Hannah Brown (11)

Ebrington Primary School, Londonderry

The Incredible Diary Of... Carla The Kitten

Dear Diary,

I was in the park with my dad who is a fireman. We were walking along when I saw a baby kitten high up in the tree. I told Dad but he just walked on. I was not going to let the baby kitten down. I kept going on about it, but he still ignored me. Why he wouldn't help me, I don't know. One night, I couldn't sleep. I was so worried about the poor kitten. Surely, it wouldn't take much to help it. "That's it," I said to myself. I had an idea.

The next day, me and Dad went back to the park. Hopefully, my plan would work. Then I shouted, "Dad, the kitten!"

He looked at me. I wasn't sure what this meant. Shockingly, my plan worked. Dad picked up his phone and called his work pals. He told me they would be here soon. Hooray! Dad looked at me with a look and I just walked on happily. Finally, they arrived. I told them where it was. They put out their ladder and climbed up. They came down with a tiny, cute and young kitten. We took her home and looked after her. I named her Carla.

Jessica Hockley-Crockett (10)

Ebrington Primary School, Londonderry

HazelTastic Adventure

Dear Diary,

Today I was going to my granny's house, but I didn't know her well because I had never met her. I was playing basketball when the ball rolled into a bush. Everyone told me to get it, so I did. As I reached in to grab it, I fell down a hole. It was full of random things, like sweets, rainbows and unicorns. When I hit the bottom, I said, "Where am I?"

I saw almost 100 doors, but couldn't get in any of them. After searching for a while, I found a small door which I crawled through. When I got up, it was a magical heaven! I saw unicorns with rainbow monkeys and even dancing Oreos! They called me over so I went and did some dancing. I was so happy when I saw singing rainbow drops. I sang for hours and hours, until I realised it was dinner time. I went to the Rainbow Gumdrop Cafe and had some colourful muffins. I then went to a clown show but it wasn't very good because only one clown showed up. The clown was sad, so I cheered him up by doing a strange dance. After a long day, I went home.

Hazel Stephanie Louise Hamilton (10)

Ebrington Primary School, Londonderry

The Incredible Diary Of... The Unliked Teddy

Dear Diary,

12:30pm

Today I got lost. I don't think my owner meant to leave me behind. She was at the arcade and set me down to play a game. Then her mum called her and she ran to her. As you can probably guess, she left me behind.

1:15pm

Some other children came past, picked me up and one said, "Ew! Who would want this as a toy?" Just as he said that, my heart dropped. I felt amazingly sad. I looked in the glass window of the game and thought maybe he was right, maybe I was ugly. Nearly every family that saw me said the same thing as that child.

1:45pm

Another person came over, she looked really, really mean. The girl took me outside and threw me on the ground. I felt a thousand times worse than I did before.

1:55pm

Then I heard a noise. Yes! Yippee! It was my owner. She had come back for me. I can't help think about what the other children had said. I think you should treat toys the same way you would treat people.

Kizzy Harvey (10)

Ebrington Primary School, Londonderry

The Magic Homework

Dear Diary,

I had a bad day in school but it was the same as every day, except my homework. But I will tell you about my day first. I got bullied again and sat on the floor again at lunchtime. But, it got so much better!

After school I did my homework and guess what happened? I wrote 'Please help me', in my book and it did my homework. Then I wrote, 'I want to be popular in school' and the next day I sat with the cool kids and they didn't do anything. In my book, I wrote, 'I want to be rich', and guess who picked me up in a very big, expensive car with a driver? It was my dad. He gave me a crown, it had gold and diamonds in it. I thought he was a king but he wasn't. He was a multimillionaire! He owned a mansion. That night, I threw my book in the fire. I whispered, "Thank you!"

Cameron McArthur (10)
Ebrington Primary School, Londonderry

The Incredible Diary Of... My Life

Dear Diary,

My name is Joelle Joanie Siwa and I am an American dancer, singer, actress and YouTuber. I cannot wait because today I'm going on tour. I cannot wait to perform in Australia I went into my room put my clothes on and then put my bow on, now I'm ready to go on tour.

Dear Diary,

I arrived at the place I am going to perform and there were thousands of fans. That just makes me more and more excited. I forgot to tell you at the start, my nickname is JoJo Siwa.

I went into my dressing room and it was spectacular. I put on my
performance costume and it was so, so pretty and then I went on stage. My first song was 'Bop' and that's also my favourite song.

After the concert I got pictures with my fans.

When I got home from that concert I was so tired. I got into my PJ's and then went to bed and was watching my videos.

My mummy came with my dinner, it was a unicorn stew. I ate it all and then I got into bed and dreamt about my next concert. I can't wait.

Tierna Cora Power (10)

Gaelscoil Na Móna, Belfast

The Diary Of Jesy Nelson

Dear Diary,

My name is Jesy Nelson and this is the diary of my life.

Today, I'm getting ready for a concert. If you have not noticed by now, I'm in a band and its name is Little Mix. I am in it with three other girls, their names are Perrie Edwards, Jade Thirlwall and Leigh-Anne Pinnock. My mum, Janice White and dad, John Nelson will be there for support with my two brothers and one sister. I cannot wait.

Okay, so I just got off the bus and I am on my way to... Sorry, I was interrupted by a fan that wanted my autograph. She was so nice so I gave her it. Now, back to what I was saying.

I'm on my way to my dressing room. OMG! It is so big, now this is exciting. I have an hour to get ready before I have to go on stage. Okay, I am dressed, now it's time to go on stage. I will be back when it's over.

Dear Diary,

It's over now, I am getting ready to go, but first I will tell you about it. There were over a million people there. I had a solo and I thought I did it well.

The other girls were even better though. It was the best night ever.

Angela-Louise Conlon (11)
Gaelscoil Na Móna, Belfast

Marshmello's Ultimate Fall

Dear Diary,

I just had my hundredth concert and it was amazing. I gained almost two million subscribers in one day on YouTube! It was amazing, the crowd screamed, I loved it and can't wait until my next one.

Dear Diary,

Okay it's been about six days since my last concert and we are in Northern Ireland, Belfast and there are so many cars parked in the parking lot. I'm teaming up with Cool FM radio, they gave me the chance to come here. Thank you so much, Cool FM, you guys are amazing.

We are about to start the concert. OMG, the music is starting! Everyone is singing, this is awesome, the singer is singing 'Happier'. I'm enjoying this so much. I'm so happy that everyone is enjoying this as much as I am.

Wow! He is really good at singing. My life is the best! I'm even doing a concert in a fortnight.

Dear Diary

So it's been a couple of days since that concert and all my concerts are being cancelled! Even my

Fortnite concert is cancelled and I'm so sad and I'm losing subscribers. I need to do another concert and I *will* succeed!

David McDermott (11)
Gaelscoil Na Móna, Belfast

The Incredible Diary Of... Ariana Grande

Dear Diary,

My name is Ariana Grande-Butera. My name was originally inspired by Princess Oriana from 'Felix the Cat'. I have an older half brother, Frankie Grande who is an actor, dancer and producer. My parents are Joan Grande and Edward Butera. I was born on 26th June 1993 and I am twenty-five years old. I'm also an actress in 'Sam and Cat', 'Victorious, 'Scream' and loads more. My saddest moment was when I was on tour in Manchester when we were bombed. Lots of people didn't survive.

I was so happy to see the people who were on their feet standing on the stage on the 'X Factor'. I've been so happy since Pete Davidson came into my life and that we became engaged in 2014, we were on our second date. But Pete Davidson and I called off the wedding because we both weren't ready!

They all say that I am worth $50 million.

When my mother was pregnant with me we were still in New York, but then we moved to Florida. Then my mother and father divorced. My father moved back to New York.

All over the world, people are going around saying the worst things about Ariana Grande, which is not true. I became famous hosting as Valentine in the hit Nickelodeon television show 'Victorious'. I'm also going on tour to the American Airlines Arena and the Staples Centre on 25th October 2019.

Cassierose McCoubrey (10)
Gaelscoil Na Móna, Belfast

The Incredible Diary Of...

Dear Diary,

My name is David Walliams. My new book is coming out, it's called 'Toothbrush On The Loose'. Anyway, I will tell you about my experience on 'Britain's Got Talent'.

Firstly, I saw a sixty-seven year-old man fit in a blue and white shoebox. Everybody laughed. After that, I was shocked, because a little blonde girl blew the biggest bubble from gum ever. Then she gave us bubblegum to chew.

A little while later another act came on and guess what it was? A talking water bottle. It opened its mouth quickly, "Hello, I'm Wally the water bottle." I was just sitting there watching carefully so I didn't miss the act. The bottle started talking again. "I have a bucket of sand." Everybody clapped Wally. There was a break, so I drank my cup of tea and ate my Maltesers. After the break we all sat down again. We looked at the bright stage, there was one bad act, he didn't really show his talent. We all looked a bit disappointed, so we waited for the next act, it took a really long time. It was a magician, he kept pulling out cards like *Bop, Pop, Wap!* We sat for hours watching the acts. I lifted up a pencil and started writing notes. The acts went on all day.

I was tired when I got home, I sat down in my armchair with a cup of tea and chocolate. It had been a long day. I was thinking about what happened. I will write again tomorrow. Bye!

Chloe Martin (10)

Gaelscoil Na Móna, Belfast

Jacqueline Wilson, A Day In The Life Of...

An extract

Dear Diary,

My name is Jacqueline Wilson and today I am ten years old. I usually get a birthday card sent in the post from my mum. Today, however, I didn't get one. I am upset but I can still just look in my size seven shoebox that I have got to put all my belongings in, like cards, underwear and pages from books my favourite authors have written. I would love to become an author. Every day I look at the five different pages and dream.

Claire and Dave called me down and surprised me with chocolate cake and tea. They got me a journal that I am using right now as my diary. Sorry Diary, I forgot to tell you my favourite author is called Enid Blyton. She's written that many books that we've had to go to the library every week for a whole year. I am definitely not complaining because my walks to the library are so much fun.

Each week I go on a different adventure. Last week I passed the park and set myself a goal. The goal was to get to the very top of the red ruby climbing frame.

This week's goal was to do a little dance step every five minutes without anyone noticing me. I am happy that it is my birthday week.

When I was three weeks old my mum put me in my dad's size seven shoebox and put me on a doorstep which belonged to Dave and Claire's auntie, Nicole. Nicole rang Dave and told him about the child in a shoebox with pages of Enid Blyton books wrapped around her. Me! Dave drove one hour to come and get me.

I love where I have grown up, but sometimes I wonder what it would have been like if I grew up with my parents...

Kyla McVeigh (11)
Gaelscoil Na Móna, Belfast

The Incredible Diary Of...

Dear Diary,

Last night was a crazy night! Let me tell you all about it.

Well, it was just like a normal night, I was getting ready for bed. Soon I was ready and went to bed. I fell asleep as usual and I was having a dream about me and my friends walking to the park. All of a sudden the ground started to shake! We all screamed and the ground pulled us apart and the sky was dark black. We couldn't see each other. It became silent, then I saw a bright light. All of a sudden I was in a big bright room. I looked up and saw some kind of blue alien monster. It took me about five seconds to realise what was going on and I waited till they left, then I crept out to the hallway and it looked like some sort of spaceship. We were in space! I was about to scream my head off, but I remembered not to or they would hear me. I didn't make a noise and an alien came up to me and grabbed me and dragged me off to eat me. They were so big, I was not wanting this to happen, so I woke up...

Ellen Archer (10)
Rathcoole Primary School, Newtownabbey

The X Factor Dance Party

Dear Diary,

Me and my friends were having a dance party. One of them filmed me and put it on YouTube.

One week later, Simon Cowell saw it and asked me to be one of the back-up dancers on the X Factor. When I found out I cried. "I can't wait to tell my friends," I said.

The next day I hopped on a plane and flew to Wembley, London. When I arrived at the arena I started to get nervous, but when I talked to a few people I felt better.

When it was time to start the show, I saw my family and friend Kiara. I felt a lot better and I started dancing to 'Survivor'.

When the song finished, I talked to Robbie Williams. But all I heard was "Wake up!"

When I woke, it was my mummy saying, "You have to go to school."

When she'd left my room, I said, "I wish that dream was real" - or was it?

Ella Conroy (11)

Rathcoole Primary School, Newtownabbey

The Incredible Diary Of... Blox

Dear Diary,

On 3rd September 2018 it was an unusual day. I just didn't know it. Myself and my friends were playing Minecraft. They started screaming! Being the sensible one I asked what was going on.

Jerry said... " You-you are Herobrine."

"What?" I said.

But Gerry went on, he said, "Bu-but you are Notch as well."

"Wait," I said.

We decided I should snap my fingers. There was a big bang! I woke up and I was in Minecraft with so many mobs on the lag. I ran, then I saw the unspeakable. I was shocked but he logged out. I looked about forever, for hours and built the best house ever.

Erin Lee McKibbin (9)

Rathcoole Primary School, Newtownabbey

The Incredible Dream

Dear Diary,

I woke up at 6am. I fell back to sleep and my dream was crazy. I was in my most played game, Fortnite. I ended it up into a solo game. I died at Top Four, sad, so I played a new match. I won, so I stopped playing Fortnite and went on Black Ops 4. I was going to play Zombies, but I played Blackout. I played fourteen matches and won ten times, so I went and played getting it to complete it twenty times. So I did complete it about forty times. Then I woke up.

Brandon Rice (10)

Rathcoole Primary School, Newtownabbey

The Incredible Diary Of... Jurgen Klopp

Dear Diary,

It has been a very eventful day. It started when I woke up in my house and was very excited. It was match day at last, a home game against Burnley in a must-win game to keep the pressure on Manchester City. I called my best players and told them that they would be starting. I visited Mo Salah instead of calling him and told him he was starting.

We arrived at Anfield at 10:30 and fans were watching us go into the dressing rooms. Burnley arrived shortly after.

When the game started the fans were singing and singing. When Burnley scored Anfield fell silent, but then Mané scored.

"Goal!"

The team were full of confidence, Salah played the ball across the box and Firmino scored.

"Goal!"

We scored two more goals and Burnley scored one. We won 4-2. The fans sang 'You'll Never Walk Alone' with their scarves over their heads.

Niall McKenna (10)

St Macartan's Primary School, Clogher

The Incredible Diary Of... Ginny Weasley: Private

An extract

Dear Diary,

I woke up this morning and had a great feeling about today. Mum called me to go downstairs to help make Harry's birthday breakfast. I put on my best robes and made my way down the stairs. Harry's presents were piled up to the roof of the kitchen.

A minute later, Harry, Ron, Fred, George, Charlie and Bill walked down the stairs into the kitchen. Mum told Harry to start opening his presents. Every time he opened something somebody spoke saying something like, "Ah, zat will give you a magnificent shave, but make sure to tell it exactly what you want, otherwise you might end up with a little less hair than you'd like."

Anyway, we had sausages and bacon washed down with coffee for breakfast. Then, after we'd finished tidying up, as we were making our way up the stairs, I called Harry. He turned around surprised and as I started to make my way to my room he followed.

As we walked in, I saw him glance around and as he glanced down at the ground I blushed, my room was a mess! Oh why hadn't I tidied my room last night?

Then there was a long, awkward silence. Harry, who like me didn't like the silence said stupidly, "Nice view."

I decided to ignore that. Then I said, "Happy birthday Harry."

Mairéad McConnell (11)
St Macartan's Primary School, Clogher

The Incredible Diary Of... Our School

Dear Diary,

I woke up and I went to school. We had a contest about our favourite author. I did mine about Jacqueline Wilson. We were sent to an author study room.

I told Mummy and Daddy when I went home, they said that that was excellent. We won a million pounds for the school.

Our school is celebrating eighty-five years this year and there are a lot of celebrations this year. There are ninety-nine pupils, four classrooms and the principal is Mrs McGinn, there are seven staff.

Our school starts at 9am and ends at 15:00. P1, P2 and P3 can go home at 14:00.

Crystal Condy (11)
St Macartan's Primary School, Clogher

The Incredible Diary Of... Rashford

Dear Diary,

On Wednesday morning, I went to Paris to play in the Stade de France in Paris. We will be playing Paris tonight to try and stay in the Champions League. Before the match started we did our warm-up, soon the match was on. I played up front with Lukaku, he scored two goals in the match and I scored a penalty in extra time. The match ended up 3-1 to Manchester United. That meant that Paris were knocked out of the Champions League. We all stayed in Paris that night.

On Thursday we went back to England. The next game is Arsenal.

Tiarnán Meehan (10)

St Macartan's Primary School, Clogher

The Incredible Diary Of... Bertie Andrews

(Inspired by 'The Butterfly Lion' by Michael Morpurgo)

Dear Diary,

My parents have just told me the white lion cub's future and mine! I feel like my heart has just been ripped into a million pieces and can never be put back together again.

Mother had a sad look on her face when I sat with her at the table. They told me the news about the white lion cub and about me going to boarding school in England! I feel a bit relieved that Mother is coming for a few months, but still, I'm not just going to let a French man who I don't even know take my lion away to a circus.

"No! No!" I told my mother and roared at father. "No! I'm going to keep my lion safe as all the other owners would."

I'm eight years old, this will be my first time on a boat and I've never even set foot outside the compound. Can my parents do this to me?

I grabbed my father's rifle and went out of the compound, my hands shaking mightily. I fired the rifle over the lion's head and as quick as a flash the lion was gone!

Fingers crossed the French man doesn't find my lion... Please, please, please!

Emma Rose Convery (9)
St Patrick's Primary School, Maghera

The Incredible Diary Of... Bertie Andrews

(Inspired by 'The Butterfly Lion' by Michael Morpurgo)

Dear Diary,

You won't believe what I am going to tell you. My father is going to send me to boarding school! My white lion cub will be sent to a circus! I feel lonely and heartbroken. I wish my father was not my father, I hate him so much today I really do. I really hope my white lion club will enjoy the circus. I don't think he will without me. I don't want the lion behind bars, I don't really trust the circus owner. I don't think the circus owner will treat the white lion cub the way it is supposed to be treated. I need to help my lion. I will not let it go to the circus and live behind bars. My lion needs its freedom before I go to boarding school and before it goes to the circus.

Dear Diary,

My lion came out of the compound, I had my father's rifle, when I shot the bullet up in the air I thought that the lion would go and it did, but it came back. I shot one more time... Away my lion

186

ran until I could see it no more...
Stay safe! God help me!

Jim Holloway (9)

St Patrick's Primary School, Maghera

The Incredible Diary Of... Bertie Andrews

(Inspired by 'The Butterfly Lion' by Michael Morpurgo)

Dear Diary,

I am going to be sent to a boarding school in England. This is thousands of miles away from Timbavati in Africa. This is the worst day of my life. I hate my father today, but the worst thing was my own white lion, who is my best friend, was going away. My father hates my white lion cub. He had arranged with a French man to take the lion to a circus. I didn't want my lion in the cage or to be hit with a whip. What a nightmare!

I don't care if they send me on a boat to England, I will miss my mummy but not my father because he is so selfish. I had to help my lion. I took my father's rifle and we sneaked downstairs and out of the compound. I had to set my lion free!

I put my arms around the lion's neck and whispered, "All my life I'll think of you. I promise I won't forget you!" Then I fired the rifle in the air to scare the lion. He ran away... It broke my heart, I will never be happy again. I will love my lion forever.

Fionn Wallace (8)

St Patrick's Primary School, Maghera

The Incredible Diary Of... Bertie Andrews

(Inspired by 'The Butterfly Lion' by Michael Morpurgo)

Dear Diary,

Today has been a tragedy. I cannot stop crying. My father told me that I have to go to boarding school, but that's not the worst... My lovely lion cub is going to the circus! The boarding school is in Salisbury in England and I have to go on a boat. My mother is going to take me and look after me in the summer, then she will leave me.

My life was going great up to now. My mother has been sad this past couple of days... now I know why. Not only am I going to England, but my lion cub is going to be sold to a French man in France.

Dear Diary,

I got my dad's gun and took it out. I took the lion out of the compound, telling him it was for his own good. I shot a bullet in the sky and my beautiful lion ran off. I don't even care if my dad straps me. I did it for my lion, he is free!

Daniel O'Kane (9)

St Patrick's Primary School, Maghera

The Incredible Diary Of... Bertie Andrews

(Inspired by 'The Butterfly Lion' by Michael Morpurgo)

Dear Diary,

This day the most terrible thing happened to me, the most terrible thing in my whole life! My dad told me that my only friend in the whole entire world, my white lion cub, would be taken away to a circus by a Frenchman. I am going be taken to a boarding school in Salisbury, England! It broke my heart completely. I was devastated, I wouldn't know what to do without him.

After I was told the news about boarding school, my dad and my mum decided that my mom could stay with me over the summer. I decided my white lion cub and I would run away out of the compound. I took my father's rifle with me. I shot in the air to make the lion run away. It didn't work the first time so I shouted at him and told him to scram. I shot another time and my lion ran free. This day was a day of hell!

Run free my lion!

Méabh Donoghue (8)

St Patrick's Primary School, Maghera

190

The Incredible Diary Of... Bertie Andrews

(Inspired by 'The Butterfly Lion' by Michael Morpurgo)

Dear Diary,

Today is the worst day of my life... I have to go to a boarding school in England. But, oh no, that is not all... My amazing lion cub has to go to the circus. It will be put behind bars! Everyone will laugh at him. My father told me this today, I feel like I might die. My mother has tried to cheer me up but it doesn't help one little bit. I hate my father, I wish he wasn't my father. I don't know what to do, should I beg father, telling him how upset I am? I will never be able to keep the lion cub. I will have to go no matter what.

I have hatched a plan, this amazing idea just has to work. I will set the lion free and the French man will *never* get my lion in his circus. I hope my lion will be safe in the wild, I pray it will all work out.

Cara Holloway (9)

St Patrick's Primary School, Maghera

The Incredible Diary Of... Bertie Andrews

(Inspired by 'The Butterfly Lion' by Michael Morpurgo)

Dear Diary,

Today my mum and dad have told me the worst news. I have to go to a boarding school in England and the worst part is my lion is being sold to a dumb circus. I will not let this man I don't know take my lion. Even if Mum and Dad don't want me to go out of the compound, I will set my lion free. I will not let him be behind bars in the circus.

My aunt and uncle are not my parents and they never will be. I don't want to go to England, I want to stay here at home, not at a boarding school. My lion can't come with me, he's like a brother to me, a brother I never had. My lion will not go to a circus even if Mum and Dad say he has to go to a circus I won't let him go... I will set him free! Tonight, I will set him free!

Annie McKenna (9)

St Patrick's Primary School, Maghera

The Incredible Diary Of... Bertie Andrews

(Inspired by 'The Butterfly Lion' by Michael Morpurgo)

Dear Diary,

My father has ruined my life! He told me that I am going to boarding school in England. He told me I need to go because a boy needs a proper education. Now I understand why my mother couldn't look me in the eye. My parents told me more bad news... That my lion was going to a circus! A French man would buy the lion for his circus. I did not want my lion behind bars and being laughed at. My father probably thinks it is best for me, but it is not!

I had a plan, I would go with my lion out of the compound and set my lion free. I got my dad's rifle from the rack. I put the rifle in the air and fired it over the lion's head. The lion scampered away... Hopefully scampered to freedom!

CiCi Murray (8)

St Patrick's Primary School, Maghera

The Incredible Diary Of... Bertie Andrews

(Inspired by 'The Butterfly Lion' by Michael Morpurgo)

Dear Diary,

I am going to school and was meant to leave my lion to a circus. My father said I was going to school and leaving the lion.

But I said, "Never!" to my dad.

I went up to my room, crying with madness. I had to do it. I took a deep breath and went down the hall. I went from the door and took my dad's gun. I went as far from the compound as I could, I sat down to get my breath back. I told the lion to stay but it didn't, it followed me.

I said, "Stay!" but it kept coming. I said, "Stay!" I got the gun and shot at it. My lion ran off into the distance... Please stay safe.

Jason Bradley (9)

St Patrick's Primary School, Maghera

The Incredible Diary Of... Bertie Andrews

(Inspired by 'The Butterfly Lion' by Michael Morpurgo)

Dear Diary,

Today is the worst tragedy in my life. My father told me that I have to go to boarding school in Salisbury in England and my lion cub had to go to the circus in France.

I was crying all night. Suddenly I had an amazing idea. In the middle of the night, I would get my father's rifle and get my lion and defend my lion. I got the lion and brought it out to the veldt, (I hope the hyenas don't eat him). I put some bullets in and aimed. I shot near an elephant, but the cub did not move. I tried again and he ran far, far away... Please God, keep him safe!

Patrick Bradley (9)

St Patrick's Primary School, Maghera

The Incredible Diary Of... Bertie Andrews

(Inspired by 'The Butterfly Lion' by Michael Morpurgo)

Dear Diary,

Today was a very bad day. My father told me that I have to go to boarding school in England. I had been crying all day long and so had my sick mother. I will travel by boat. On top of this, he said my lion had to go to a circus that the French man owned and he would put the lion behind bars. Tonight I got my father's rifle and scared my lion away. I pray he doesn't have to go to a circus where he is behind bars. I had to be careful the hyenas didn't see him.

God keep him safe!

Owen Glass (8)

St Patrick's Primary School, Maghera

The Incredible Diary Of... Bertie Andrews

(Inspired by 'The Butterfly Lion' by Michael Morpurgo)

Dear Diary,

I was having a great day until the afternoon. My father said I had to go to school. That is not all... My lion had to go to a circus! I was petrified and I'm still petrified. I can't stop my eyes from crying. I have to go to England on a boat. I was wondering why my mother was so sad.

I tiptoed down the stairs and picked up father's gun. I went outside and... The next thing I knew, *bang!* My lion was gone. My lion was free! Run lion, run lion!

Meghan O'Kane (8)

St Patrick's Primary School, Maghera

Bella The Kitten

An extract

Dear Diary,

I woke this morning and my mum and I were going to find some food for breakfast. We were getting ready to go when this cruel man set a fire. I shouted to Mum, "There's a fire over there." So we ran across the field and there were millions of cows and one of them stood on my mum. She died and I was so sad. I kept running on until all the cows went away.

A car drove by, so I decided I would follow it. The car led to a massive house and people started to get out. I ran over to a girl and she called her brother. She said, "Look at this." Then they went inside and got some food, so I went and jumped on the window and the girl said, "Go away," because her dad wouldn't let me stay there. Then another car pulled up, I think it was their mum. I felt quite sad because I didn't have any mother to hug, but I got over it.

It started to get dark, so I went over to a tree and slept there for the night. I woke up and went to the window and the girl came out and gave me some food, but she didn't tell her mother or anyone because she knew they wouldn't like it. She asked her mum if she could have me as a pet. She said no but the girl said she would feed me, make me a home and take me for walks. Her mum said she would have a chat with dad when he got back from work. The girl decided to prove to them that she could look after me. The first thing she had to do was to give me a name. She called me Bella.

Grace Connolly (9)
St Tierney's Primary School, Roslea

Life As A Pug!

Dear Diary,

It all started with me sleeping in my kennel. I was starting to wonder where my food was because I normally get it at this time. I watched and watched the kennel door and finally a man came and fed me. He didn't look like my owner, but then I ate the food anyway. I then got bored, so I went to the airport because we live near it. I am quite small, so I jumped in a hole in someone's smelly hand luggage and jumped out when they sat down, ran under the seats to the back of the plane. I then got very worried because someone was sneezing, I thought they might be allergic to me.

After about five hours I saw people coming over to the man who was still sneezing and they asked if he was allergic to anything. He said, "I am allergic to most dogs and cats."

Oh no, I said to myself.

Finally the plane stopped, so I had to get back in someone's hand luggage. I did that pretty well until the person who owned the bag opened it and saw me in it. Phew! The person loved dogs and took me off the plane and set me free. I didn't know where I was so I looked everywhere and saw a sign that said *France*.

It was very fun because I got to sunbathe and go for a swim. Finally it was time to go home so I did the same thing but without as much chaos as last time.

For some reason my owners were back when I was back. Maybe they went on a plane too!

Anna Rooney (9)
St Tierney's Primary School, Roslea

The Time Machine

Dear Diary,

I'm having a normal day farming. My friend, that I work for, told me to mow the field. I was going to the tractor. Suddenly I spotted a time machine. I pressed the button and it took me back 1,000 years. I saw very old people milking the cows, there were old, rusty tractors. I decided to have a walk around the farm to see what else I could find. I saw old men cleaning the pigpen by hand. I went into an old house and there were people knitting, it was really small. I made a few friends, their names were Jack, Jimmy and Alan.

I went back to the time machine and came back and my son was wondering where I'd been.

I said, "It is a long story."

I got back to my friend's field. Then a really bad thing happened. The mower broke down and I had to leave the tractor to go and get it fixed. It took me two hours to fix it. Then my friend came over, I mowed the rest of the field and then I got a phone call, the last thing I wanted was to slurry. I had to say no. Then I went home.

Aodhan O'Donnell (8)

St Tierney's Primary School, Roslea

202

The Incredible Diary Of... Max The Dog

Dear Diary,

I got up, then I went out to the woods and I saw a man. He said, "You look hungry, let's get you some food. You can come home with me."

I barked to say thank you.

The man took me to get some food and water, then he took me for a walk.

After that, the man got me a lovely, soft bed and I got into it.

After a while, the man went to sleep after watching TV for six hours. When he woke I was so happy because he took me to the beach. We played fetching the ball, then he took me to his mum's house.

He said, "Look Mum, I found this dog."

She petted me and said, "What a lovely dog, I will keep him."

The man said, "No, no, I can keep him. He loves me."

Then the man took me home and went to bed after my busy day.

Max the Dog

Brooklyn Fisher (10)

Thornfield House School, Newtownabbey

The Incredible Diary Of...
Princess Amelia

Dear Diary,

I woke up and got my dress on. Next, I brushed my long curly hair and got my cereal. It was Unicorn Pop cereal my big sister had Coco Pops cereal. I cleaned up my room then I helped my mummy to do the dishes. Next, I helped my daddy clean the car. Then my big sister and I picked some flowers and I played with my friends. We played tag and tip and then we played with our toys.

My dad let me and my friends plant flowers in the garden, then I played again with my friends and went for a walk with my big sister, my mummy and my daddy. We saw a rabbit and on the top of the hill we saw a deer and a bear. Then my sister and I played a game, it was tig. I went home and we watched TV and movie called 'Unicorns'.

We laid down on the grass and looked up at the sky and the clouds and then ran around the garden.

Then it was dinner time, we had a roast dinner and we ate it all up. My daddy watched the Royal

football game, I had a bath and got my pyjamas on, it was time for bed, and it was a brilliant day.
Princess Amelia

Abbie Savage (10)
Thornfield House School, Newtownabbey

The Incredible Diary Of... The Black Knight

Dear Diary,

Today I went to a Viking village. The Vikings started attacking me, so I blew my horn and then my army came to fight them. Then we took over. I went back home, then a Viking army attacked the village at my home. All the people died. I walked away from home. Then I saw a Samurai base. I saw the Viking ships at the Samurai base and there were twenty Vikings dead, killed with arrows.

I went into the Samurai base and I saw a fight with the Samurai and the Vikings. I got into the fight to and I spoke to my archer. Then arrows were fired at the Vikings and the Samurai, black slime came out of the ground. Finally, the Vikings got stuck and we were safe.

Today was a fight to the death. I hope tomorrow will be a day with no fighting.

From The Black Knight.

Zak Patterson (9)

Thornfield House School, Newtownabbey

The Incredible Diary Of... The Astronaut Who Went To Space

Dear Diary,

I always wanted to go to space in my lifetime. Now is my chance! I wanted to have time with my friends first, so we played football, we went to the arcade and I used the tickets for new headphones. The whole time I was thinking about aliens and wondering if they were real, but I knew they were not real.

Anyway, my rocket was ready, so I went to the lift and there were a lot of buttons. I heard the countdown, ten, nine, eight, seven, six, five, four, three, two, one, then blast off! *Whoosh!* I was in space. Then we had touched down and I opened the door and walked outside. It was beautiful. Then, at last, I placed a flag.

I was amazed, the real question was, "How do I get back from the adventure?"

Maksims Andrejevs (10)

Thornfield House School, Newtownabbey

Donald Duck To The Rescue

Dear Diary,

I woke up in my house, I got my breakfast, my favourite cereal, Quackers because I'm a duck. I got my hat and went off for a walk with my kids and went to the shop. After that, we went for a picnic.

Then we got into the river, but I got out for a moment because I heard there was a crocodile in the river. So I got into my helicopter and told the kids to grab a rope and they survived.

We told the police to get the crocodile into a cage.

We went back to our house, the kids were playing with the Xbox and they played Duck Games for a while. I sat in my chair to watch TV.

Today was a scary day, I hope tomorrow will be a fabulous day.

Donald Duck

Jake Whitehouse (9)

Thornfield House School, Newtownabbey

208

The Incredible Diary Of... Jack The Dog

Dear Diary,

I woke up and I went to my owner. I jumped up and I looked at him, then he got up too. We went downstairs to get food. I got my eggs and my dog food. I ate it all. My owner had toast.

Then, I went outside to go to the toilet. After I went back inside. We went into the living room and watched TV. Next, we went to the park to play a ball game. We saw another dog and another owner. The owners were talking, the other dog was playing with me. After we played my owner and I went to the shop to get food for dinner. Then we went home to get dinner and afterwards I went to bed. I hope tomorrow is a good day.

Ethan Mulholland (10)

Thornfield House School, Newtownabbey

The Incredible Diary Of... Eagle

Dear Diary,

I woke up from my sleep, I got my breakfast and after that, I went off for a fly.

I was flying in the air and found a place called the jungle. I got lost. I didn't know where to go, I was sad and lonely.

It was lunchtime, but I did not get lunch. I was so hungry and I tried to look for food but couldn't find any. Then my dad found me, I was happy he had food with him. He fed me some meat then we flew home and got some dinner.

Today was a very bad day, I hope tomorrow is better.

Eagle.

Mason Bowers (9)

Thornfield House School, Newtownabbey

210

The Incredible Diary Of... Marley The Police Officer

Dear Diary,

I was at the security area checking all of the people were behaving very well. But last night, the robbers were robbing the bank. I wanted the rest of the guards to help to arrest the robbers.

We got the robbers into jail. Today was the best day ever. I hope the robbers don't rob the bank again.

Marley, the police officer

Marley Sebastian Ludew (10)

Thornfield House School, Newtownabbey

Young Writers Information

We hope you have enjoyed reading this book – and that you will continue to in the coming years.

If you're a young writer who enjoys reading and creative writing, or the parent of an enthusiastic poet or story writer, do visit our website **www.youngwriters.co.uk**. Here you will find free competitions, workshops and games, as well as recommended reads, a poetry glossary and our blog. There's lots to keep budding writers motivated to write!

If you would like to order further copies of this book, or any of our other titles, then please give us a call or order via your online account.

Young Writers
Remus House
Coltsfoot Drive
Peterborough
PE2 9BF
(01733) 890066
info@youngwriters.co.uk

Join in the conversation!
Tips, news, giveaways and much more!

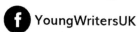 YoungWritersUK    @YoungWritersCW